The Ultimate SCIENCE COOKBOOK for Kids

Official Kid Testers:

Lila M., age 13

Oliver P., age 9

Josie P., age 11

Official Kid Tester Lila Mozingo, age 13, with her Speedy Snacks!

SCAN HERE TO SEND US YOUR PHOTOS.

Highlights.com/ShareCookingPics

SCAN ME

Highlights

The Ultimate
SCIENCE
COOKBOOK
for
Kids

75+
Edible Experiments

HIGHLIGHTS PRESS
Honesdale, Pennsylvania

Table of Contents

DRINK IT!
78–93

COOK IT!
94–109

PLAY WITH IT!
110–129

MODEL IT!
130–145

RE-CREATE IT!
146–155

* =  QUICK AND EASY

Let's Cook Up Some Science!

DID YOU KNOW?

A hot pepper isn't actually burning your mouth—it just tricks your brain into thinking your mouth is on fire! Find out more about **spice science on page 35.**

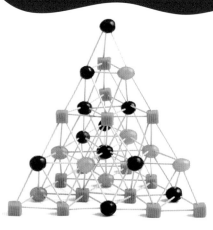

Triangles are one of the strongest geometric shapes! Find out why and build cheese-and-grape structures using **triangle formations on page 12.**

Ever wanted to make a drink in all the colors of the rainbow? Discover just how delicious density can be and make **Rainbow Limeade on page 92.**

Put on your apron and grab your beakers— it's time to experience some cooking and science fun!

Cooking and science go hand in hand. After all, cooking is really just one big science experiment! This cookbook brings all the joys of cooking and the fun of science to a whole new level. Every recipe in this book gives you a chance to whip up something tasty while learning about food science, astronomy, chemistry, biology, and more! Even better, the book offers lots of ways to experiment with the recipes you're cooking up so you can give each dish your own spin. Whether you're an expert chef, a cook in training, or a scientist extraordinaire, we promise you'll find something to love (and to learn) in every recipe!

Safety Tips!

Be safe while cooking up fun! Read the directions for each recipe and activity carefully. **Follow these safety tips:**

Wash your hands with soap and water before you get started and after touching anything raw.

Always remember to turn off the stove when done.

Ask a grown-up for help with anything sharp or hot.

If you have long hair, tie it back.

Use oven mitts for hot pots and pans.

And if you have any questions along the way, ask a grown-up for help.

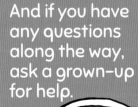

BUILD IT!

If you like making towers of toy bricks and enjoy engineering, this is the chapter for you.

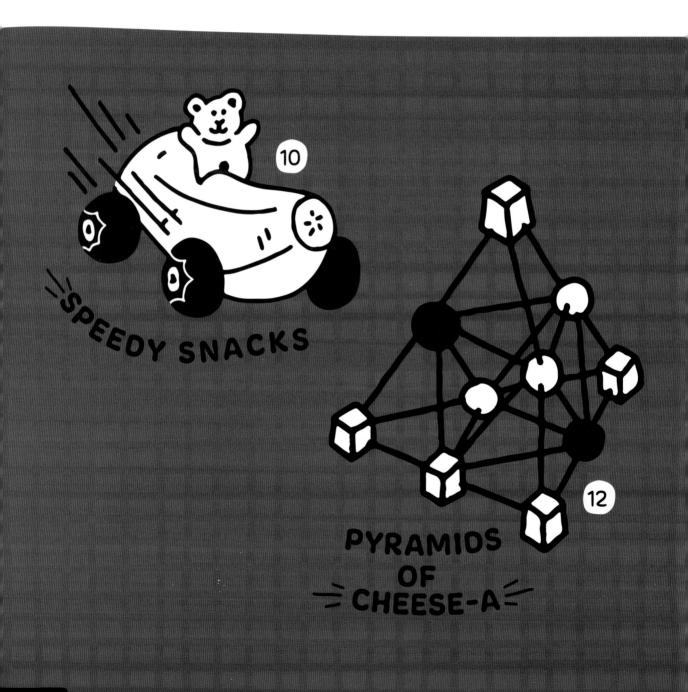

SPEEDY SNACKS — 10

PYRAMIDS OF CHEESE-A — 12

PRETZEL ROD BRIDGE (14)

(16) **FRUIT KEBABS**

(18) **MARSHMALLOW DINOS**

SPEEDY SNACKS

Build an edible car and learn how wheels work. Use toothpicks and cream cheese to assemble your fruit-and-veggie vehicles.

You Need

- ▸ Fruits
- ▸ Veggies
- ▸ Toothpicks
- ▸ Cream cheese

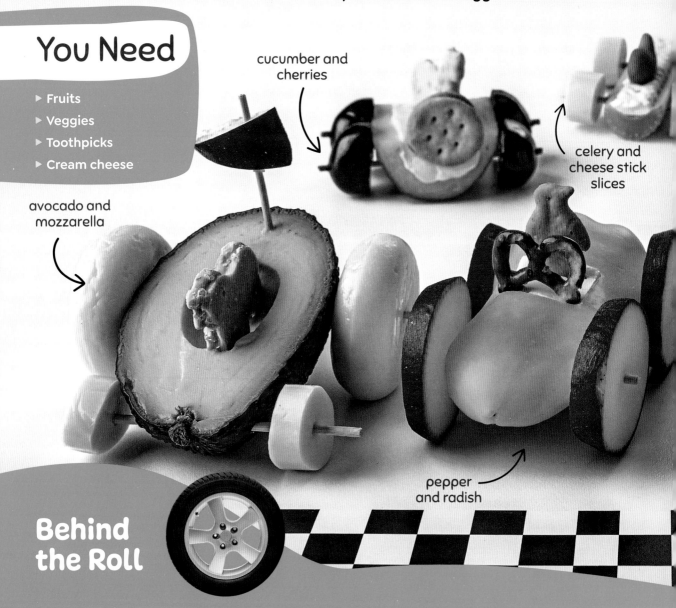

cucumber and cherries

celery and cheese stick slices

avocado and mozzarella

pepper and radish

Behind the Roll

Here's a wheel-y cool part of a vehicle: the wheel! Wheels are simple machines that can help move heavy items by rolling them along the ground. This simple machine contains two main parts: a wheel and an axle. The axle is a type of pole placed through the open center of a wheel or multiple wheels. And this axle is attached to the vehicle. Cars and other vehicles usually have at least two axles—one for each set of wheels. A car's wheels are able to spin around its axles, keeping the car in constant motion.

As the wheels move, they encounter something called friction. Friction is a force that

Build two cars and race them across a clean surface! Which goes faster? Why?

pepper and cherries

banana and blueberries

For extra fun, add a driver or steering wheel!

pepper and cucumbers

orange and grapes

happens when one object slides or moves over another. This force acts against, or resists, movement. In the case of a moving car, friction occurs between the tires on the wheels and the ground. The friction isn't strong enough to completely stop a vehicle. But it keeps tires from slipping on the road. Friction also helps a car come to a halt. To stop their car, drivers press down on the brake. This brake controls a brake pad that presses against the moving wheels. The action produces enough friction to bring the wheels to a controlled stop.

PYRAMIDS OF CHEESE-A

Using just toothpicks, grapes, and cheese, try building a pyramid that rivals one of the wonders of the world.

You Need

- ▶ Toothpicks
- ▶ Cheese, cut into large cubes
- ▶ Red and green grapes

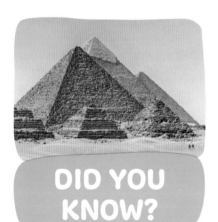

DID YOU KNOW?

The Pyramids of Giza were built 4,500 years ago—and they're still standing! Made from more than two million stone blocks, they were built as tombs for Egyptian pharaohs.

1. Using grapes, cheese cubes, and toothpicks, create a line of flat triangles. Each triangle connects to the one next to it with a shared cheese cube or grape. For each triangle you add, the pyramid will get bigger.

2. Connect a second row of flat triangles to the tops of the triangles in row 1. Each new row should be 1 triangle shorter than the last. Continue adding rows with this same method, until it makes one big triangle. This will be the base of the pyramid.

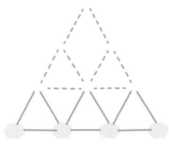

3. Use 3 toothpicks to create a pyramid on each little triangle in the base. Only build pyramids on the triangles that are pointing upward, not the ones pointing downward.

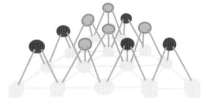

4. Connect all the pyramid tops with toothpicks. For the best result, this layer of the structure should be completely flat, and the outside edges should be perfectly straight.

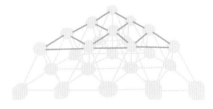

5. Repeat steps 3 and 4, adding rows of mini pyramids and connecting them, until you reach the top of the big pyramid.

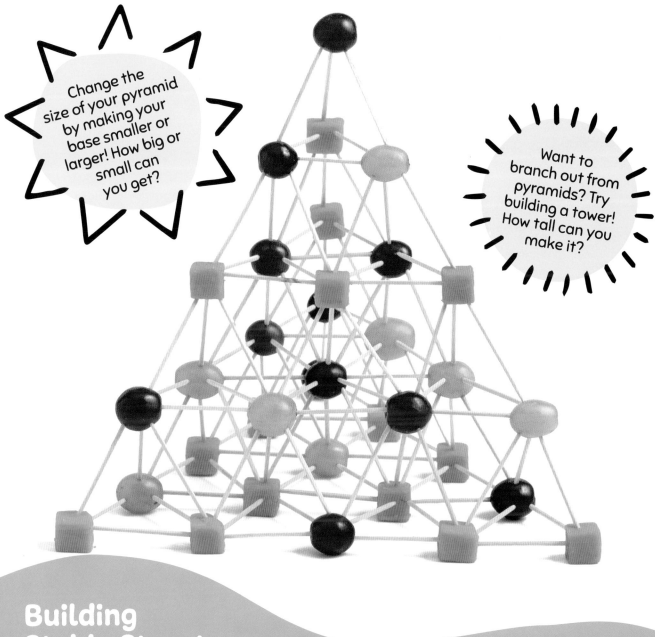

Change the size of your pyramid by making your base smaller or larger! How big or small can you get?

Want to branch out from pyramids? Try building a tower! How tall can you make it?

Building Stable Structures

The triangle is one of the strongest geometric shapes that can be used to construct a building. A triangle is made of three parts that all lean on and support one another. Plus, weight placed on the triangle will spread out evenly over all the triangle's sides. This means that the triangle is less likely to fall over. So

why aren't most buildings shaped like triangles? This is because it is easier for people to live in large, open spaces made of squares and rectangles. However, architects can still use smaller, triangle–shaped building pieces to add extra support and stability (and style!) to their structures.

Builders also use strong materials like steel and reinforced concrete. And every building has an inner structure called a frame that gives it shape and support, sort of like how your skeleton gives you shape and support. No bones about it—that's cool!

PRETZEL ROD BRIDGE

Create a stable truss bridge using pretzels and science!

You Need

▸ Pretzel rods
▸ Royal icing mix (stiff)
▸ Ruler or measuring tool

1. Bridge Deck:

a. Place 2 full pretzel rods parallel to each other on parchment paper, about 2 inches apart.

b. Prepare icing according to box instructions. Put it in a resealable plastic bag and cut a piece from the corner. Pipe a thick line of icing across the length of each rod.

c. Cut other pretzel rods into 2- to 3-inch pieces. Stick the pieces across the icing-topped rods. Let sit for 45 minutes or until dry.

2. Two Trusses:

a. For each truss, cut 10 2-inch pretzel pieces from rods. Make sure the edges are flat and all pieces are roughly equal in size. Add a glob of icing on top of each pretzel piece. Take two additional full rods, and "glue" 5 of the smaller pieces to each, as shown below. If needed, add more icing on the seams.

Glue after cutting

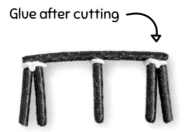

b. Without "gluing," place a pretzel rod diagonally between each of the truss edges to estimate the size of the piece. Cut. Remeasure and adjust as needed. Then "glue" it down.

c. Let sit until dry enough to flip over. Add more icing to the seams on the back side of each truss. Let sit for 20 more minutes or until completely dry.

3. Assemble:

a. Ask someone to hold each dry truss upside down while you pipe a glob of icing on all the bottom pieces. Turn the trusses right side up, and then "glue" each to one side of the deck, adding more icing to the seams as needed. Add a can or something supportive from the kitchen to hold up the trusses as they dry. "Glue" pretzel pieces across the top.

Place rod here

Cut rod where it touches center piece

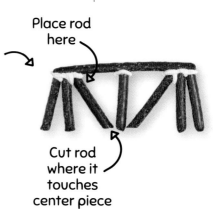

Balance your bridge across two objects. How many orange slices can it hold?

Safety Tip!
Have an adult cut pretzels by sawing them with a serrated knife.

How Do Bridges Hold Weight?

To carry lots of people, cars, and more every day, a bridge must balance two different forces caused by gravity and weight: compression and tension. Compression is a force that pushes or squeezes inward. Tension is a force that stretches or pulls outward. To prevent the bridge from breaking, architects have to figure out how to get rid of these forces or to spread them out evenly.

Almost all bridges use abutments and piers to do this. Abutments are supports that sit at the ends of a bridge. They help direct weight and pressure to the ground on either side of the bridge instead of onto the bridge itself. Piers are supports in the middle of a bridge. These channel pressure directly down into the ground.

Some architects also create truss bridges (like the pretzel rod bridge in the activity on the previous page). These are bridges supported with frames made of strong materials. The frames can be built from vertical and diagonal bars that help support the bridge and distribute force.

FRUIT KEBABS

Make kebabs with strawberries and other fruits
and then extract DNA from leftover strawberries!

You Need

RECIPE
- Kebab sticks
- Fruits

EXPERIMENT
- Rubbing alcohol
- Strawberries
- Resealable plastic bag
- 1 teaspoon dish soap
- ¼ teaspoon salt
- Coffee filter
- Funnel
- Clear glass cup
- Pipette or eyedropper (optional)
- Magnifying glass (optional)

DID YOU KNOW?

Strawberries are the only fruit with seeds on the outside of their skin. Each strawberry has approximately 200 seeds.

watermelon

grape

strawberry

Strawberry DNA Experiment

1. Chill the rubbing alcohol in the freezer until it is cold (approximately 10 minutes). While it is cooling, prepare the strawberries by pulling off any leaves or stems.

2. Place the strawberries in the plastic bag. Push out the air in the bag and then seal it. Next, use your hands or a rolling pin to smash the strawberries into mush.

3. Add dish soap, salt, and ¼ cup water to the bag. Seal the bag, shake well, and then set it aside for 5 minutes.

4. Line the funnel with a coffee filter. Place the funnel in the tall glass. Carefully pour ⅛ to ¼ cup of the strawberry mixture into the coffee filter in the funnel. Wait about 4 minutes, then pick up the filter and gently squeeze it so that excess liquid is strained through the filter and into the funnel. Be careful not to pop the filter by squeezing it too hard.

5. Add about an inch of the chilled rubbing alcohol to the glass.

6. A thick, soupy material should rise to the top of the alcohol. This is strawberry DNA! If you want, use the pipette or eyedropper to pull out a little of the DNA and place it on a clean towel or plate. Use your magnifying glass to check it out!

How does it work?

Delicious DNA

Every living thing on the planet—including plants and their fruits, like strawberries—is made up of at least one tiny, living unit called a cell. Most organisms are made from many cells! Each of these cells has microscopic, threadlike structures called chromosomes. Chromosomes consist of something called DNA. DNA acts as the blueprint—or the instructions—for each living creature, determining traits such as size, coloring, and more. Human cells each have two copies of a person's DNA. But a strawberry's cells each have eight copies of its DNA! This makes it easier to extract, or take out, the DNA to study it.

By mushing up the strawberries, you begin to break them down into their individual cells. Adding the dish soap, salt, and water helps break down the fruit further so that the strawberry DNA is released into the solution. The salt helps keep the strawberry DNA from dissolving in the water. The rubbing alcohol makes the DNA strands rise together to the top. Now you can check them out!

MARSHMALLOW DINOS

Think you can build a perfectly balanced dinosaur?
Try it out with this engineering challenge.

You Need

- ▶ **Large marshmallows**
- ▶ **Small marshmallows**
- ▶ **Paper straws**
- ▶ **Scissors**

1. Look at a picture or toy of a *T. rex*. Notice that it walks on two feet.

2. Brainstorm ideas for building a model of a *T. rex* out of marshmallows and straws. (You can cut the straws with the scissors to make them smaller.)

3. Your dinosaur must have a body, head, tail, arms, and legs. And it must be able to stand on its own.

How Did Dinosaurs Stay Balanced?

To stay balanced, all dinosaurs—whether they were big or small, or walked on two legs or four—most likely relied on their tail. This is similar to how many four-legged animals today balance. For instance, researchers have found that cheetahs use their tail to help keep their balance as they run, and even to turn very fast.

By relying on computer simulations, scientists have been able to model how many dinosaurs might have moved their tail while they walked. In fact, it seems that many two-legged dinosaurs actually wagged their tails to keep steady while they moved.

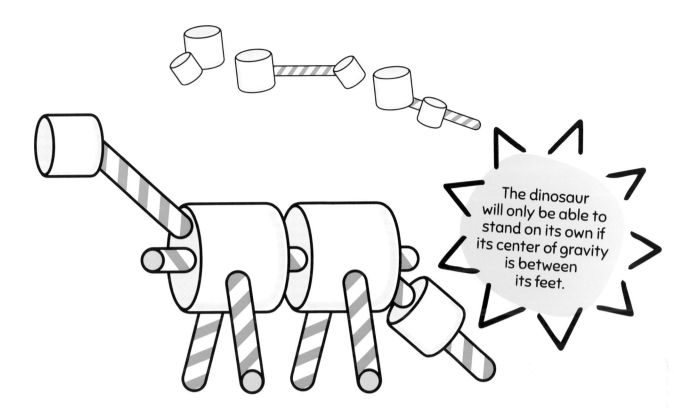

The dinosaur will only be able to stand on its own if its center of gravity is between its feet.

4. Once you succeed, look at a picture or toy of a *Brontosaurus*. Notice that it walks on four feet.

5. Consider ideas about how you can transform your model to represent this kind of dinosaur. You can use additional straws and marshmallows.

6. It must have a body, head, tail, and legs, and it must be able to stand on its own.

How does it work?

The force of gravity pulls things toward the center of Earth. The center of gravity is the point where a body is in balance. If a body (or a dinosaur!) is not in balance, gravity will cause it to fall over.

A two-legged dinosaur's arms also helped it stay upright. Some two-legged dinosaurs, like *T. rex* and *Carnotaurus sastrei*, evolved to have large heads but very short arms. They likely used these little clawed arms to slash prey for dinner. Short arms may have also helped make these dinosaurs less heavy toward their fronts, which prevented them from toppling over.

TASTE IT!

Want to try a mishmash of all things food science? Check out this chapter.

22 ENERGY BITES

24 BAGEL BONANZA

26 DEVILED EGG DELIGHTS

28 APPLE DIPPERS

30 BRAVE FLAVORS

32 PASTA SALAD

SPICY SALSA DIP 34

GET TOASTY 36

ROCK CANDY

38

BANANA TREATS 40

CHEESY NIBBLERS

41

YOGURT STIR-INS

42

ENERGY BITES

Power up with an oaty snack and learn
how our bodies convert food into energy!

You Need

- ▶ 1 cup rolled or old-fashioned oats
- ▶ ½ cup nut butter
- ▶ ⅓ cup honey
- ▶ Pinch of salt
- ▶ Your favorite flavor mix-ins
- ▶ Parchment paper

1. In a large bowl, combine oats, nut butter, honey, and salt.

2. Stir in your favorite flavor additions.

3. Roll into balls and place on parchment paper.

4. Decorate with toppings if you wish.

5. Chill in the fridge or in a covered container.

apple chunks

stomach

intestines

How Do Our Bodies Convert Food into Energy?

Your body starts digesting food as soon as you put it in your mouth. Saliva, or spit, has special substances called enzymes that begin to break down your meal. After you have chewed, your tongue helps push the food to the back of your throat.

When you swallow, the food enters a pipe called the esophagus. Muscles in your esophagus squeeze the food down toward your stomach. Next, muscles in your stomach and a fluid known as gastric acid help turn the food into liquid mush. This mush enters your small intestine. Now, your body can start to turn that food into energy.

The food you ate contains nutrients like carbohydrates, fats, and proteins. Your body breaks these nutrients apart to create new energy!

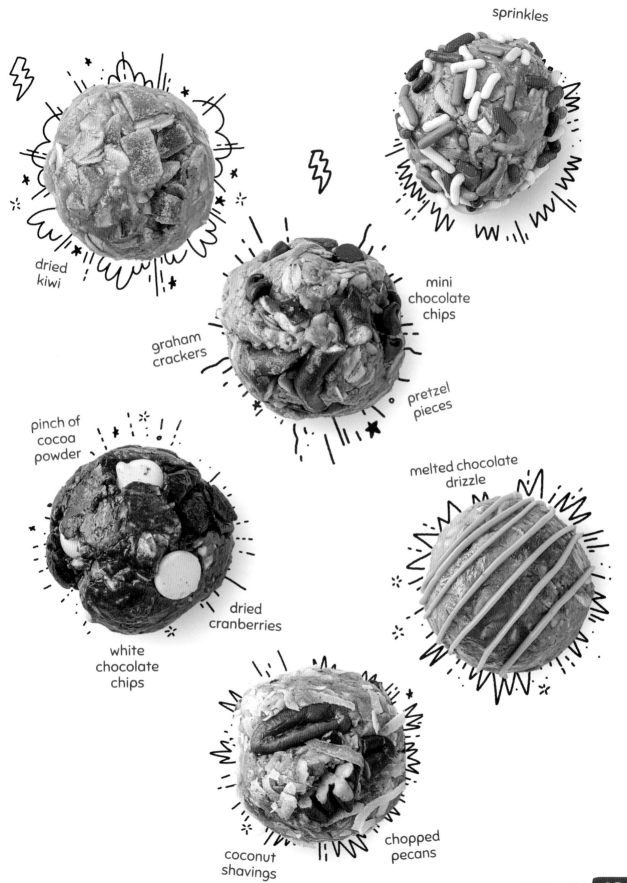

dried
kiwi

sprinkles

mini
chocolate
chips

graham
crackers

pretzel
pieces

pinch of
cocoa
powder

melted chocolate
drizzle

dried
cranberries

white
chocolate
chips

coconut
shavings

chopped
pecans

BAGEL BONANZA

Add some delicious toppings to a bagel and discover the hole-some history behind this baked delight.

You Need

▸ Bagel
▸ Your favorite toppings

Tasty Tuna

sesame bagel

red onions

tuna salad

lettuce

DID YOU KNOW?

Bagels are boiled before they are baked because it helps seal in the dough's starch and make a thicker crust. All of this creates a chewier cooked bagel.

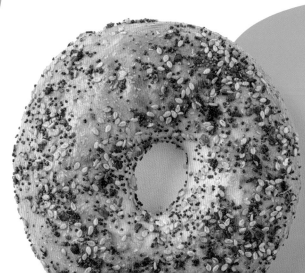

Why Do Bagels Have Holes?

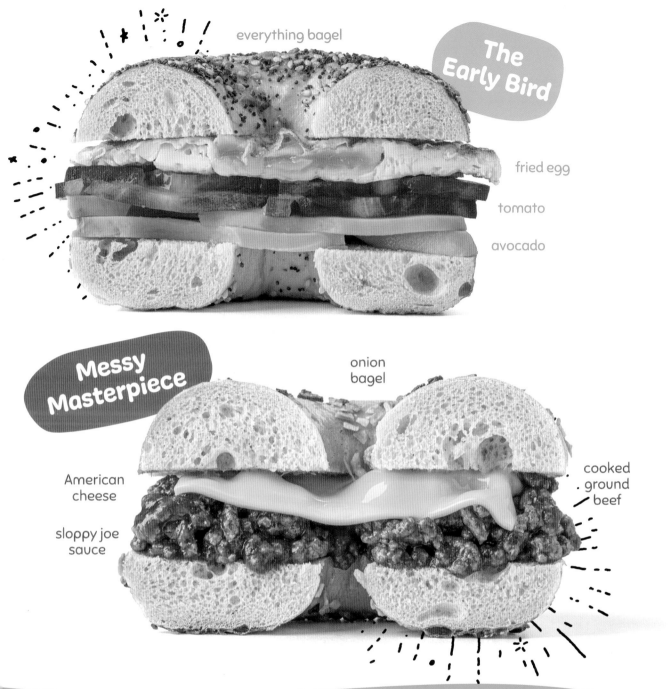

everything bagel

The Early Bird

fried egg

tomato

avocado

Messy Masterpiece

onion bagel

American cheese

sloppy joe sauce

cooked ground beef

To make a bagel, a baker kneads a special mixture of dough and shapes it into a ring. Then, the baker boils the dough ring in water and bakes it in the oven. During the cooking process, the bagel's hole increases something called surface area. Surface area is the amount of space that makes up the face, or the outside, of an object. A larger surface area means that the bagel will have more of that tasty crust. It also means that the bagel will cook more evenly. Imagine a bun with no hole. In that case, the heat needs to travel all the way through the bun, starting from the crust and traveling inward. So it takes longer for the inside of the bun to cook than the outside. But with a hole, the heat can travel through dough from different points. This keeps the dough soft, fluffy, and evenly baked.

DEVILED EGG DELIGHTS

Experiment with boiled eggs to learn about density.
Then make delicious deviled eggs with them!

You Need

RECIPE
- Eggs, boiled
- Your favorite flavor mix-ins

EXPERIMENT
- Two identical tall cups
- Water
- Salt
- Eggs, uncooked

Floating Egg Experiment

1. Fill two identical tall cups about three-quarters of the way with water. Add the salt to one glass. Use a spoon to stir it until the salt dissolves completely.

2. Gently drop one egg in each glass. What happens?

Boats, hot-air balloons, and even icebergs float because of buoyancy.

How does it work?

Density Eggs-travaganza

When you place a whole uncooked egg in plain tap water, the egg sinks. This is due to something called density. Density measures how tightly particles, or tiny pieces of matter, are packed into a substance. When you place an item in water, two forces act on it: buoyancy and gravity. Buoyancy is what causes an object to float in water. Gravity pulls the object down (see page 93). A raw egg has more density than plain tap water. This means that the gravity on the egg will be stronger than its buoyancy, and the egg will sink. But something changes when you add salt. By dissolving the salt into water, you add more matter to the same amount of space. Now, the salt water is denser than the raw egg—increasing the buoyancy and pushing the egg up. This causes the egg to float!

Now boil the eggs until hard and make deviled eggs out of them!

Cut a hard-boiled egg in half. Scoop out the yolk. Mix it with a tiny bit of the filling items.

Spoon the yolk mixture back into the egg whites, and add toppings.

Everything and More
FILLING:
mashed avocado
lime juice

chopped tomatoes

bacon bits

everything bagel seasoning

Wing-a-Ding
FILLING:
mayonnaise
chopped celery
white vinegar
wing sauce

chopped chives

blue cheese

Taste of Tzatziki
FILLING:
plain Greek yogurt
chopped garlic
lemon juice
fresh dill

The Double Dare
FILLING:
sriracha
lime juice
mayonnaise

crushed spicy cheese snacks

feta cheese

chopped cucumbers

APPLE DIPPERS

Make yummy dipped apples with melted chocolate candies.
Then find out what makes certain foods, like melted chocolate, sticky.

You Need

- ▸ Apple
- ▸ Wood lollipop sticks
- ▸ 1 cup candy melts
- ▸ 1 teaspoon shortening
- ▸ Your favorite toppings
- ▸ Parchment paper

Purple Crisp

sprinkles

1. Wash an apple. Twist off the stem. Poke a lollipop stick into the bottom of the apple.

2. In a small microwave-safe bowl, mix 1 cup candy melts (available in many colors in craft stores) with 1 teaspoon shortening. The mixture should be deep enough to cover the entire apple.

3. Microwave on half power for 1 minute. Stir. Add 30 seconds, if necessary.

4. Dip the apple into the mixture and quickly sprinkle on toppings.

5. Let the apple dry on parchment paper.

Choco-Mallow Chomp

dehydrated marshmallows

hot cocoa mix

Coconut Craving

coconut flakes

sprinkles

What Makes Some Foods Sticky?

What makes foods like melted chocolate, peanut butter, marshmallows, honey, and more naturally sticky? They're made of molecules, tiny building blocks of matter that like to stick to one another and to other surfaces. When an item sticks to itself, it's called cohesion. When it sticks to something different, it's called adhesion. There are some foods that have lots of cohesion and adhesion.

Whenever you eat, the saliva in your mouth quickly breaks apart the molecules in the food (see page 22). But most naturally sticky foods tend to absorb lots of water. This means that rather than being worn down, the food simply soaks up the fluid. But stick with it! Eventually, the stickiness will subside with more saliva.

BRAVE FLAVORS

Try some wacky flavor combos as you learn why certain foods taste so good together.

You Need

ICKLE-PICKLE SANDWICH
▸ Bread roll
▸ Pickles
▸ Peanut butter

FRUITY MAC SNACK
▸ Mac and cheese
▸ Apples

SPICY-SWEET TREAT
▸ Ice cream
▸ Spicy rolled corn chips

bread roll

Ickle-Pickle Sandwich

pickles

peanut butter

The Scoop on Taste

What makes certain unexpected food pairings taste so good? The answer comes down to how—and why—we taste. A human's tongue is covered in tiny bumps called papillae. The bumps contain small organs known as taste buds. Taste buds allow you to sense flavor: when your taste buds touch food, tiny hairs on the taste

Fruity Mac Snack

mac and cheese

apple chunks

spicy rolled corn chips

ice cream

Spicy-Sweet Treat

Make other wacky combos using your favorite flavors. What funny dish did you come up with?

buds send signals to your brain to process the taste. Humans likely developed the ability to taste different things to help us seek out the nutrients we need. Being able to taste means that we're able to recognize nutrient-rich food. We can also stay away from bad-tasting foods that might make us sick. Sometimes, pairing unexpected flavors together—such as sweet and sour, or savory and sweet—can create balanced but exciting combinations that taste extra delicious to us.

PASTA SALAD

Make delicious pasta salads. Then discover why pasta softens when it boils.

You Need

- ▶ Pasta
- ▶ Your favorite salad dressing
- ▶ Your favorite toppings

chipotle ranch dressing

green onions

Rodeo Roundup

wagon wheel pasta

corn

red bell peppers

Behind the Boil

When cooking a pasta dish, a lot of people use pasta that has been dried, or dehydrated. Drying pasta makes the noodles easier to store and sell, and helps the pasta keep its shape. Pasta noodles are filled with a type of molecule (or tiny building block) called starch. Starch holds a lot of water. When pasta makers want to dehydrate pasta, they leave the noodles out to dry. Over time, the water in the

Try some of these flavor combinations.

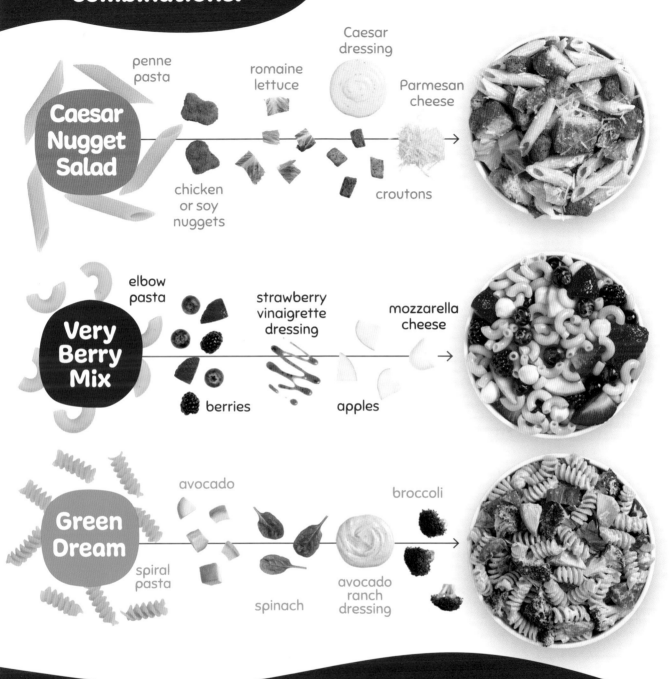

Caesar Nugget Salad
penne pasta · chicken or soy nuggets · romaine lettuce · Caesar dressing · croutons · Parmesan cheese

Very Berry Mix
elbow pasta · berries · strawberry vinaigrette dressing · apples · mozzarella cheese

Green Dream
spiral pasta · avocado · spinach · avocado ranch dressing · broccoli

starch evaporates, or turns from a liquid into a gas. But that means to cook the pasta, water must be added back in—in other words, it needs to be rehydrated. To do this, pasta is boiled in water. As the pasta sits in the water, the starch molecules absorb moisture again, becoming softer and more flexible. The longer you leave noodles in the water, the more moisture they absorb—and the softer they get. At the same time, the heat of the boiling water transfers to the noodles, making them warm. Bon appétit!

SPICY SALSA DIP

Make salsa, add it to a layered dip, and then find out what makes some foods spicy.

You Need

RECIPE

- ½ cup diced sweet bell pepper
- ½ cup diced tomato
- ¼ cup diced red onion
- 1 tablespoon chopped cilantro or parsley
- 1 tablespoon lime juice
- 1 teaspoon olive oil
- ½ teaspoon sea salt
- ½ cup roasted tomato puree
- 1 finely diced garlic clove
- 2 teaspoons diced jalapeño pepper
- ½ cup peeled and diced cucumber
- Hot sauce (optional)
- Sour cream
- Guacamole
- Refried beans
- Tortilla chips

EXPERIMENT

- Cilantro

1. In a small bowl, combine the bell pepper, tomato, red onion, and cilantro. Mix together with lime juice, olive oil, and salt.

2. With an adult's help, use a food processor to blend the tomato puree, garlic, and jalapeño pepper. Add the mixture to the bowl and stir in the cucumber.

3. For more zing, add a few drops of hot sauce.

Soapy Cilantro

For some, cilantro tastes zesty and fresh. For others, eating cilantro is like biting into a bar of soap! Why? Some people carry a gene that brings out cilantro's soapy taste. Before adding cilantro to your salsa, nibble on some to see if you have this gene!

Now, make a layered dip with your salsa!

➡ In a small bowl, add layers of your favorite dip ingredients.

➡ Top with your homemade salsa and use tortilla chips to start scooping!

tortilla chips

salsa

sour cream

guacamole

refried beans

What spicy (or mild) foods would you include in a layered dip?

Why Are Some Foods Spicy?

Have you ever wondered why some foods give your mouth that burning feeling? This is thanks to a substance called capsaicin, a chemical in some foods like hot peppers. Cells in your mouth react to capsaicin. Cells are small, living units that make up your body. They can interact with each other—and with the outside world—and send information to your brain. When the cells in your mouth interact with capsaicin, they send a signal to your brain that creates a "burning" feeling. Your mouth is not really burning, but because of the capsaicin, your brain thinks it is! Scientists believe that over time, some plants evolved using capsaicin as a way to discourage other animals from eating them.

GET TOASTY

QUICK AND EASY

Try this trick to keep avocados from browning.
Then create the perfect avocado toast.

You Need

RECIPE
- Toast
- Hummus
- Avocado
- Your favorite toppings

EXPERIMENT
- Ripe avocado
- Lemon or lemon juice

Don't Go, Avocado
Experiment

1. Have an adult cut both the avocado and lemon in half. Use the spoon to scoop out the avocado pit. Leave the avocado skin intact. Then squeeze the juice from both halves of the lemon (or ¼ cup lemon juice) into the small bowl. Add ½ cup water to the bowl.

2. Place half of the avocado face down in the bowl with the lemon juice and water mixture. Place the second half face up on the plate.

3. Let both halves sit at least 8 hours and up to 24 hours. Think about what each avocado half might look like later.

4. Once the wait time is up, examine the avocado halves. How are they different?

How does it work?

Bring on the Brown

You may notice that the avocado half on the plate turned a light brown. When an avocado is cut open, oxygen interacts with the flesh of the fruit normally hidden under skin. This flesh contains substances called enzymes, which begin to interact with oxygen when exposed to air. Together, the enzymes and oxygen make new, harmless chemicals. However, as part of this process, they also create something called melanin, the substance that gives things their color. Melanin is even in your skin and hair! The melanin produced during this interaction between the avocado and air happens

Want more avocado? Try making the perfect avocado toast.

What other toppings could you add to avocado toast?

bread

everything bagel seasoning

avocado slices

garlic hummus

to look brown. This is called enzymatic browning.

Enzymatic browning is very common and can also happen to other fruits like apples, pears, and bananas. It might not look pretty, but it's completely harmless, and you're free to snack away. However, you can stop—or at least slow it down—the enzymatic browning. You probably saw that the avocado half in lemon juice did not turn brown. That's because lemon juice contains acid, which slows down the chemical reactions in the fruit by preventing the enzymes from working as quickly.

ROCK CANDY

Grow edible crystals from sugar!

You Need

- **2 cups sugar plus a few tablespoons**
- **3 wooden skewers, trimmed to about 6 inches**
- **3 heatproof jars or glasses**
- **Food coloring (optional)**
- **Flavor extract, such as vanilla or peppermint (optional)**
- **Spring-loaded clothespins**
- **Masking tape**

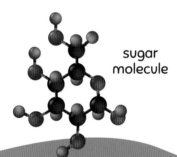

sugar molecule

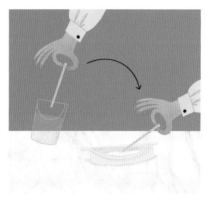

1. Pour a few tablespoons of sugar onto a plate. Dip the end of each skewer into water. Roll the end of the wet skewer in sugar. Coat only the bottom inch or two. Set the skewers aside to dry on a wire rack.

2. Fill the jars with hot water and set aside.

3. Boil 1 cup water in a saucepan. Add 1 cup sugar. Stir slowly and carefully. Once dissolved, add the second cup of sugar and stir again. Bring to a boil and simmer for a minute or two. Remove from heat and let cool for 20 to 30 minutes. The liquid should still be warm.

Growing Candy

How does it work?

This simple candy has a trick that's not so simple: it grows by itself!

To make rock candy, you dissolve sugar—lots and lots of sugar—into hot water. Sugar dissolves in water because the tiny parts—or molecules—of the water break up the molecules of the sugar. This process happens quickly when the water is hot, as heat makes the molecules work much faster.

For rock candy, so much sugar has to be dissolved into the water that it creates a saturated solution. This is when the maximum amount of one substance has been dissolved into another, meaning absolutely no more sugar could be dissolved into the hot water.

Because of how fast its molecules move, hot water can hold more dissolved sugar

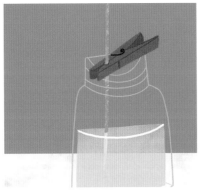

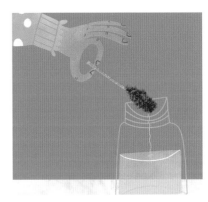

4. Empty the water out of the jars. Add a few drops of food coloring and flavoring to each jar if you want. Have an adult pour the warm sugar solution into each jar. If you need to, stir to combine.

5. Attach a clothespin to the top of each skewer. Balance the clothespins on the tops of the jars. The skewers should hang straight down with the end of each skewer about a half inch above the bottom of the jar. Tape the clothespins and skewers in place if they are wiggly.

6. Place the jars in a safe spot that doesn't get hot or sunny. Wait 5 to 14 days, until rock candy forms on the end of the skewer. Then break the crust at the top of the jar, pour out the extra liquid, and remove the candy. You may need to set the jar in hot water to warm it up before you can pull out the candy.

than cool water. But when the saturated solution starts to cool, it won't be able to hold as much dissolved sugar. That sugar will have to find somewhere to go.

When you leave a wooden skewer in the saturated solution, that is where the extra sugar will head. As the solution cools and evaporates, molecules of sugar start to form solids again, which cling to each other and to the skewer. This forms sugar crystals. As evaporation continues over time, these sugar crystals will attract more sugar, and more crystals will grow until your stick is covered in hardened sugar—rock candy.

BANANA TREATS

QUICK AND EASY

Try the banana writing experiment at the bottom of the page, then use the banana to test some new flavor combos.

You Need

RECIPE
- ▸ Bananas
- ▸ Your favorite toppings

EXPERIMENT
- ▸ Banana
- ▸ Toothpick

Cool Mint

Cucumber and mint

PB & H

Peanut butter and honey

Orange Crush

Orange piece and coconut flakes

Rad Red

Cherries and chocolate

How does it work?

Banana Writing Experiment

1. With permission, use a toothpick to write on an unpeeled banana.

2. Wait a few minutes and observe the banana. What happens?

You should notice that within minutes, the damaged part of the banana skin will darken. As most bananas ripen, their peels turn from green to yellow to brown because of how the substances in them called enzymes interact with the air. If you cut the peel, it starts to brown almost immediately. Damaging the peel makes the enzyme actions happen more quickly. In time, the whole banana will rot because its protective peel was damaged. But you'll have eaten the banana long before that happens!

QUICK AND EASY

Take a bite out of these cheesy treats and learn how this dairy delight is made.

You Need

▶ Fruit
▶ Vegetables
▶ Cheese

Crunchie Munchie

Colby Jack cheese and celery

Tangy Cuke

Goat cheese and cucumber

Cheesy Chomp

Cream cheese and apple

Say Cheese!

Humans have been making cheese for thousands of years. Today, cheesemakers start by pouring milk into a large container known as a vat, then add special kinds of bacteria and enzymes. This begins the process of breaking down the milk into yogurt (see page 42). However, cheesemakers don't stop there. Over time, the milk separates into thicker, yogurt-like solids and the remaining liquid, called whey. Cheesemakers then remove the whey and heat the thick solids to let out even more whey. They press the remaining solids together and mold them into blocks. These blocks are left to age and continue to ferment. Cheesemakers can make different types of cheese—including ones that taste stronger or milder, and ones that feel firm or soft—depending on how long they let them ferment.

(see page 42)

YOGURT STIR-INS

Learn how to make Greek yogurt from regular yogurt.
Then add some delicious toppings.

You Need

RECIPE
▶ Yogurt
▶ Your favorite toppings

EXPERIMENT
▶ Regular yogurt
▶ Coffee filter

 DIY Yogurt Experiment

1. Place a mesh strainer over a bowl.

2. Line the strainer with a coffee filter.

3. Pour regular yogurt into the coffee filter.

4. Let it thicken in the fridge for approximately 6 hours or longer for thicker results.

5. Scoop the Greek yogurt out of the strainer and notice the layer of clear whey at the bottom of the bowl.

How does it work?

Making Yogurt

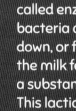

Scientists think that humans first made yogurt more than 7,000 years ago in what is now the Middle East—and people have been making it the same way pretty much ever since! Yogurt makers begin by heating milk (most often from a cow, goat, or sheep). They then add special types of healthy bacteria to the warm milk, along with substances called enzymes. Over time, the bacteria and enzymes break down, or ferment, the milk. As the milk ferments, it produces a substance called lactic acid. This lactic acid gives yogurt its creamy texture and tangy taste. After the lactic acid forms, most of the liquids (known as whey) are strained from the solids in the mixture, creating regular yogurt. And, as the experiment above shows, Greek yogurt is regular yogurt that has been strained of *even more* liquid, making it even thicker and creamier. Now that's yummy!

Now add some mmm-mmm-good toppings to your Greek yogurt!

salsa and tortilla chips

chickpeas and pesto

sliced strawberries and sprinkles

cereal and crushed pineapple

BAKE IT!

If you like the classics and want to learn about the chemistry of baking, this chapter is a great place to start.

BAKED BREAD & GRILLED CHEESE 46

FROZEN YOGURT BAKED ALASKA 48

MAPLE OAT COOKIES 50

PANCAKE TACOS 52

54 PEPPERMINT MELTAWAYS

56 SOLAR APPLE S'MORES

58 JUMBO DOUGHNUT CAKES

60 BANANA BREAD

BAKED BREAD & GRILLED CHEESE

Give the science of bread baking a try and make an ooey, gooey grilled cheese with the results!

You Need

- 3½ cups all-purpose flour, plus extra for dusting
- 1 packet instant/fast-acting yeast
- 1 teaspoon fine sea salt
- 2 tablespoons vegetable oil, plus more for greasing
- 1⅓ cups warm water (120–130°F)
- Your favorite grilled cheese toppings

2. Make a well in the middle and add oil and water. Use a spatula to mix everything together. As the dough forms, use your hands to make it into a soft, sticky ball.

4. Place the dough ball in a greased bowl and turn the ball to coat it in oil. Cover with a damp kitchen towel and let it rise in a warm spot for 1 hour, or until doubled in size.

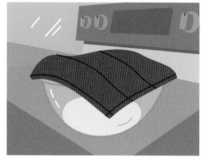

1. Whisk together flour, yeast, and salt in a large mixing bowl.

3. Dust your hands and a clean countertop with flour. Place the dough on the counter and knead until it is smooth and holds together in a ball. To test, poke it with your finger. If the dough bounces back, it's ready.

5. Place the dough on the counter again. Press and pull the dough into a rectangle. (It doesn't have to be perfect.) Starting at the short end, roll the dough into a log. Tuck the ends under and press the dough seam side down into a greased pan.

Use your bread to make grilled cheese! We added mac and cheese. What will you add?

6. Cover with the towel and let it rise for 1 hour, or until the dough has risen 1 inch above the pan's rim.

7. When the dough is almost finished rising, place the rack in the lower one-third of the oven. Bake at 400°F for 25 to 35 minutes or until golden brown. Let the bread cool in the pan for at least 5 minutes. Using oven mitts, remove the bread from the pan and set it on a wire rack.

How does it work?

Yeast is a tiny, single-celled organism. It's actually a type of fungus!

The Lowdown on Bread Rising

To make bread, bakers combine flour and water to create a dough. They add salt for flavor and yeast, then mix the dough with their hands in a process known as kneading. The yeast starts to break down, or ferment, the natural sugars in the flour. When the sugars break down, they release carbon dioxide. This gas becomes trapped within the sticky, stretchy dough, creating bubbles inside the mixture and causing the dough to rise. Heat from the oven causes the carbon dioxide to expand, making the bread rise even more. This gives the baked bread a fluffy quality.

FROZEN YOGURT BAKED ALASKA

Cooking frozen yogurt? That's right! It can be done melt–free with the power of science.

You Need

- Plastic wrap
- Frozen yogurt
- Pound cake
- 3 large egg whites
- ½ teaspoon cream of tartar
- ¾ cup sugar
- Parchment paper

1. Line a large bowl with plastic wrap. Allow the frozen yogurt to sit at room temperature for 10 minutes, until softened.

2. Scoop the frozen yogurt into the plastic-wrapped bowl, pressing down firmly to fill any gaps.

3. Cut the pound cake into 1-inch-thick slices. Place the pound cake slices in an even layer over the frozen yogurt, trimming the slices, as needed, to fill any gaps.

4. Cover the top of the bowl with plastic wrap and freeze for 4 hours, or overnight, until the frozen yogurt and cake are firm.

5. Make the meringue topping by whisking egg whites and cream of tartar in another large bowl. With an adult's help, beat the egg white mixture using an electric mixer, until foamy. Keep beating as you sprinkle in the sugar. Stop when the mixture is fluffy and stiff.

6. Flip the cake onto a rimmed baking sheet lined with parchment paper. Remove the bowl and plastic wrap. Spread the meringue evenly over the cake. Using the back of a spoon or spatula, create peaks. With help from an adult, toast the meringue under the oven broiler on the bottom rack for 1 to 2 minutes, until toasted.

How does it work?

Hot Outside, Cool Inside

Even though you've placed scoops of frozen yogurt in a hot oven, it doesn't melt—but how? The science behind this neat trick is called thermal insulation. Thermal insulation refers to a material or technique that keeps heat from spreading. Thermal insulation is important in many homes; it helps keep heat out in the hot summers and keeps warmth in during cold winters. Materials used in thermal insulation are ones that heat does not move through easily. As it turns out, air is a great thermal

Use your favorite frozen yogurt, ice cream, or dairy-free creamy treat!

insulator! Think about when you wear a simple jacket. It is not the material of the jacket that keeps you warm; instead, the jacket traps warm air around your skin. This is sort of what happens with the baked Alaska—but in reverse! When you made the meringue, you whipped a lot of air into the egg whites. Then, the stiff, air-filled egg whites acted as a protective dome in the oven, trapping in the cold air and keeping the heat away from the frozen yogurt.

MAPLE OAT COOKIES

Bake up some maple oat cookies and then experiment with leftover maple syrup.

You Need

RECIPE

- ▶ 1 very ripe banana
- ▶ 1 large egg
- ▶ ¼ cup maple syrup
- ▶ 1½ cups quick oats
- ▶ ½ cup pecans
- ▶ 2 tablespoons dark brown sugar
- ▶ 1 teaspoon baking powder
- ▶ ½ teaspoon ground cinnamon
- ▶ ⅛ teaspoon salt
- ▶ ½ cup raisins

EXPERIMENT

- ▶ ½ cup pure maple syrup

1. Preheat the oven to 350°F. While the oven preheats, mash a ripe banana in a large bowl.

2. Mix egg and maple syrup with the mashed banana.

3. Add oats, pecans, brown sugar, baking powder, cinnamon, and salt. Mix well. Then fold in raisins.

4. Line a baking sheet with parchment paper. Use a ¼ measuring cup to scoop the batter onto the parchment paper. Flatten the cookies with the back of a spoon. Bake for 15 minutes or until firm and cooked through. Cool before eating.

No pecans? Try ¼ cup sunflower seeds instead!

For more maple goodness make maple syrup crystals!

Maple Syrup Crystals Experiment

1. Place a baking sheet in the freezer so that it becomes very cold. (Or, if it's snowy outside, gather some clean snow and pack it onto your baking sheet.)

2. Pour maple syrup into a saucepan. With an adult's help, heat the maple syrup over medium-low heat on the stove. Carefully stir the maple syrup for about 10 minutes. The syrup should bubble, thicken, and become foamy.

3. Take the saucepan off the stove and set it aside. Remove the chilled baking sheet from the freezer. With an adult's help, carefully dribble the maple syrup onto the cold baking sheet in circles (or a design of your choice).

4. Wait 5 to 10 minutes. The maple syrup should harden into crystals. (If the crystals are not hardening or are taking too long, place the sheet back in the freezer.) Use a spoon or spatula to lift the crystals off the pan and give it a taste!

How does it work?

It takes about 40 gallons of sap from a maple tree to make just one gallon of maple syrup!

Maple Molecules

Maple syrup is sticky, oozy, and gooey. So how did it turn into firm crystals? This has to do with the molecules in the maple syrup. Every substance in the world is made up of different chemicals. The chemicals themselves are made up of teeny-tiny units called molecules. Maple syrup consists of water and sugar. When you boil the maple syrup, heat changes the water molecules from a liquid into a gas. This is called evaporation. Now, there is more sugar than water. However, the heat makes the molecules in the sugar very active. This causes them to bounce around, making the syrup stretch out in a liquid. To make the syrup into a hard candy, you need to cool it. Cooling the sugar molecules makes them move slower. Now, they move closer together, joining into a firm (and tasty!) candy.

PANCAKE TACOS

Make pancake tacos and learn all about gluten.

You Need

- ▶ Pancakes (premade or homemade)
- ▶ Your favorite toppings

chocolate pancake

coconut shavings

Cocoa Taco

strawberry slices

whipped cream

Behind the Stretch

Pancakes aren't just delicious. They are also floppy and flexible enough to fold up like a taco. So, what is it that makes pancakes—and other types of bread—so stretchy?

Most breads, pancakes, and pastries are made of flour from wheat or other grains. Many of these grains contain two proteins known as glutenin and gliadin.

When bakers add water or milk to the flour and mix the ingredients together, the proteins combine to form a network of protein molecules known as gluten. This protein network is stretchy and springy—it gives noodles their bounce and pizza crust its stretch. The more the batter is mixed, the more gluten forms, meaning the mixture will be stretchier.

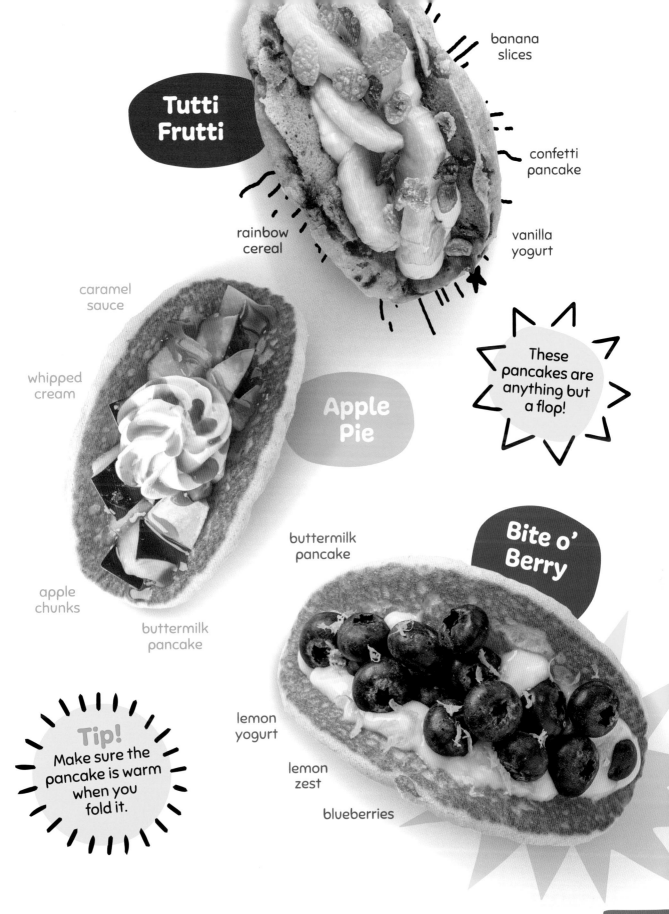

Tutti Frutti

banana slices

confetti pancake

vanilla yogurt

rainbow cereal

caramel sauce

whipped cream

Apple Pie

These pancakes are anything but a flop!

apple chunks

buttermilk pancake

buttermilk pancake

Bite o' Berry

lemon yogurt

lemon zest

blueberries

Tip! Make sure the pancake is warm when you fold it.

PEPPERMINT MELTAWAYS

Is that a chill in the air or is it just mint? Whip up this cool concoction and discover the truth behind peppermint's ice-cold flavor.

You Need

- ▶ Aluminum foil
- ▶ 8 egg whites
- ▶ ½ teaspoon cream of tartar
- ▶ ¼ teaspoon salt
- ▶ 1 cup granulated sugar
- ▶ 2 cups powdered sugar
- ▶ 1 teaspoon vanilla extract
- ▶ 1 teaspoon peppermint extract
- ▶ Food coloring

1. Preheat the oven to 250°F. Line baking sheets with foil. Combine the room-temperature egg whites, cream of tartar, and salt. With an adult's help, beat with an electric mixer until foamy.

2. In a separate bowl, mix together the granulated and powdered sugars. Add the sugar mixture a little at a time to the eggs as you continue to beat them. Add vanilla and peppermint extracts. Beat for about 10 minutes.

3. Swirl in a few drops of food coloring. Spoon dollops onto the baking sheets.

4. Bake for 1 hour until the cookies are cream-colored. Turn off the oven. Leave them inside overnight without opening the door.

Try This!
Dip the cookies into melted chocolate and decorate with sprinkles.

DID YOU KNOW?

The ancient Romans used mint to freshen up their baths and perfumes.

Why Does Mint Taste Cold?

Mint and mint-flavored foods are famous for being cool, refreshing, and crisp. But unlike other chilly snacks and beverages—such as ice cream or cold drinks—mint isn't cold to the touch. In fact, if you hold a mint leaf or a piece of mint-flavored gum in your hand, it will probably feel room temperature. Yet once you put it into your mouth, your mouth might start to tingle or go numb. Why is that? All over your body—including inside your mouth—you have cells that are designed to send messages to your brain about how hot or cold something is, what it tastes like, what it feels like, and more. But when these cells come into contact with a certain chemical found in mint, they get confused.

Although mint isn't actually chilly itself, it contains a chemical that tricks your mouth into feeling cold. This chemical is called menthol. When your cells encounter menthol, they react the same way that they might if you were to touch an ice cube or something else chilly— by sending signals to your brain that you are touching something cold! This means that when you chew on mint and release the menthol inside, your brain interprets this menthol as chilly. *Brrr!*

SOLAR APPLE S'MORES

Use rays from the sun to create a tasty, toasted treat.

Solar Oven Experiment

You Need

- Aluminum foil
- Graham crackers
- Chocolate
- Large marshmallow
- Magnifying glass
- Apple slice

1. Set up a small table or chair outside in the sun. This will be your workstation.

2. Tear off a piece of aluminum foil about 6 inches long. Fold the aluminum foil in half, and then unfold the foil.

3. Start piecing together your first s'more by stacking one graham cracker, a square of chocolate, and a marshmallow on one half of the aluminum foil.

4. Fold the other half of the foil so that it directs the sun's light onto the marshmallow.

5. Hold the magnifying glass between the foil and the marshmallow to turn up the heat.

6. When the marshmallow is toasted, add an apple slice and another graham cracker to the s'more and enjoy!

No time for a sun-cooked s'more? Cook the marshmallow in a microwave, oven, or campfire!

Safety Tip!
Wear sunscreen and only direct the magnifying glass's light onto the marshmallow.

graham cracker

marshmallow

chocolate

apple slice

How does it work?

Cooking with the Sun

By the time the sun's heat reaches Earth, it isn't hot enough to toast a marshmallow all on its own. But with a magnifying glass and some foil, you can change that! A magnifying glass helps focus and increase the sun's heat. Normally, the sun's energy travels in large waves. The lens of the magnifying glass directs many of these waves into one place. With all that energy in one spot, it starts to get hot—really hot! The aluminum foil also reflects the heat around the s'more, causing the ingredients to become nice and soft.

JUMBO DOUGHNUT CAKES

Learn to make this cakey creation, then find out the secrets behind cake baking.

You Need

- 2 ring pans
- Cooking spray
- Flour
- Cake batter (from a box or make your own)
- Your favorite toppings

If cake batter is under-mixed, not enough air will be added to the batter. This makes the cake denser and more crumbly.

Cake Cooking Experiment

1. Grease and flour the ring pans.

2. Prepare 2 boxes of cake mix—or your favorite cake batter recipe—in 2 separate bowls. Leave one under-mixed and mix the other one all the way.

3. Pour the batters into separate ring pans. Bake according to the instructions on the box or in the recipe.

4. Once the cakes have finished baking and cooled in the pans, ask an adult to carefully remove the cakes from the pans and put them on a serving plate. Notice how the two cakes look different because of how well they were mixed.

5. Decorate the cakes to look like giant doughnuts!

Sugar and Spice

cinnamon sugar

spice cake

The Science of Cake Baking

When you bake a cake, every ingredient is important. Some are there to taste good. But others undergo or counteract specific chemical reactions that will make the dessert bake correctly.

Many of these reactions happen when heat is introduced during cooking. A reaction that happens thanks to heat is known as an endothermic reaction. To understand more about

how different ingredients react to heat or how certain ingredients impact the reactions between heat and other ingredients, think about what would happen if you—whoops!—forgot to include

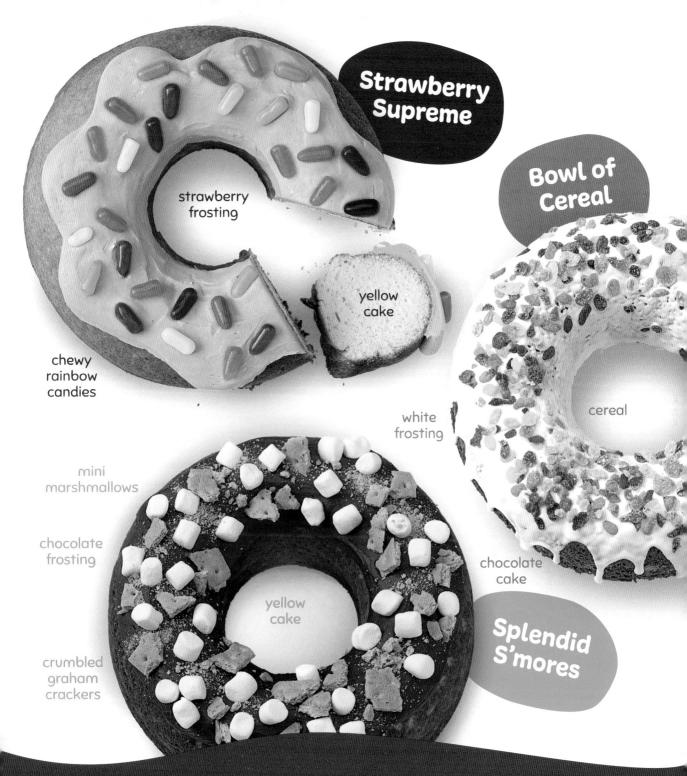

Strawberry Supreme

strawberry frosting

yellow cake

chewy rainbow candies

Bowl of Cereal

cereal

white frosting

chocolate cake

mini marshmallows

chocolate frosting

yellow cake

crumbled graham crackers

Splendid S'mores

something from the recipe. Take oil, for example. Oil is a type of fat. When a cake is baked, the heat evaporates most of the moisture—except for the oil. Without this ingredient, the endothermic reaction of evaporation can dry out the cake. Baking powder is a special type of acidic chemical. When it encounters heat, it releases a gas called carbon dioxide, which helps the cake rise. Without baking powder, the cake can be sunken or flat. All of these reactions prove the old saying: Baking really is a science!

BANANA BREAD

Experiment with ripening fruit and make banana bread with the result.

You Need

RECIPE
- ⅓ cup butter
- 4 ripe bananas
- 1 egg
- ¾ cup sugar
- 1 teaspoon vanilla
- 1 teaspoon baking soda
- ¼ teaspoon salt
- 1½ cups flour
- Vegetable oil spray

EXPERIMENT
- 2 green bananas
- 2 brown paper bags
- 1 apple

1. Preheat oven to 350°F. Melt butter in a bowl. Peel a banana and slice into chunks if it's not already mushy. Put the banana in a large bowl and mash it. Stir in the melted butter.

2. Crack an egg into a small bowl. Beat the egg with a fork.

3. Add beaten egg, sugar, and vanilla to the banana mixture. Stir in baking soda and salt.

4. Mix in flour. Spray a loaf pan with oil and pour the mixture in. Bake for 1 hour. Cool on a rack before removing bread from the pan.

Take your banana bread to the next level by adding a handful of chocolate chips or some nuts.

Got green bananas? Try this experiment to get them to ripen more quickly!

What happens when you put a banana and an orange in the same bag? An orange and an apple?

Ripen Bananas Faster Experiment

1. Put one banana in each bag.

2. Place the apple in one of the bags. Close both bags.

3. Observe both bags every day for a week. Take notes on or draw pictures of what you see.

4. Which banana ripens faster?

DID YOU KNOW?

Bananas are actually berries! Bananas are formed from only the female part of the flower. And every banana has a soft inside with tiny seeds that you may not notice. Because of these characteristics, botanists consider bananas berries.

How does it work?

Rapid Ripening

As they start to ripen, fruits like bananas and apples produce a gas called ethylene. The bag with two pieces of fruit had more ethylene trapped in it, so that banana ripened more quickly. Not all fruits are like this, though—some, like oranges and grapes, don't continue to ripen after they're picked.

DECORATE IT!

If you love to get artsy and express your creativity, this chapter will be your favorite!

CUCUMBER BOATS 66

CELERY SNACKS 64

SHARING BOARDS 68

70
GLOW-IN-THE-DARK GELATIN

72
WHAT'S POPPIN'?

74
STICKY TREAT SUSHI

VEGGIE INSECTS

76

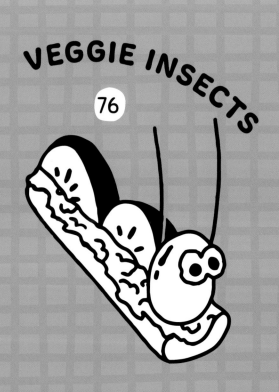

CELERY SNACKS

QUICK AND EASY

Do an experiment with celery, then top the leftovers with cream cheese and other foods.

You Need

RECIPE
- ▶ Celery
- ▶ Cream cheese
- ▶ Your favorite toppings

EXPERIMENT
- ▶ 2 celery stalks with the leafy tops still attached
- ▶ Food coloring

Colorful Capillaries Experiment

1. Fill each glass about halfway with water.

2. Squirt a different color of food coloring into each glass, using at least 5 drops for each. Use a spoon to stir each glass.

3. Break off the bottom edge of each celery stalk.

4. Place a stalk of celery in each glass. Leave the celery for at least a day. What do you see?

How does it work?

Changing Colors

In this experiment, the food coloring should move up the celery stalks and into the leafy tops. This process is called capillary action, which is a liquid's ability to travel upward, against gravity, in narrow spaces. In plants, capillary action helps water climb from the roots all the way to the highest leaves. Water that has been pulled into the celery leaves evaporates, leaving behind a colorful dye. Once this water has left the plant, the stalks pull more water into the leaves, adding additional color to them.

Now, make some crunchy celery snacks with the unused celery!

Using a spoon or butter knife, fill your celery sticks with cream cheese.

Add your favorite toppings and experiment with different flavor combos!

Chutney Chomp

apple-cranberry chutney

Pepper Perfection

sliced red bell pepper

dried cranberries

Grape-o-rama

sliced grapes

Cool Cranberry

crumbled bacon

halved blueberries

Blueberry Blitz

sliced olives

Bring on the Bacon

O-mazing Olive

CUCUMBER BOATS

Create cucumber boats and learn why fruit and veggie skins are so good for you.

You Need

- 1 (5-oz.) can of tuna
- Mayonnaise
- Relish
- Carrot shavings
- Cucumber
- Toothpicks
- Salt
- Pepper

1. Mix drained tuna and mayonnaise in a bowl. Stir in relish and carrot shavings.

2. Cut the cucumber lengthwise. Scoop out the insides of the cucumber sections to make the boat bases.

3. Spoon the tuna mixture into the cucumber boats.

4. With an adult's help, shave an extra slice of cucumber with a potato peeler. To create a sail, poke a toothpick through the slice. Add to the boat. Add salt and pepper to taste.

Super Skins

The outer part of a vegetable or fruit—known as the peel or skin—acts as a tough layer that helps protect a plant from sun, rain, insects, and more. Many people peel off the skin to get at the softer, juicier inner parts. But as it turns out, the skin packs a super healthy punch! For one thing, skins are often the part of the plant with the darkest coloring. The chemicals that cause these colors are full of antioxidants, which help protect the plant from pollution. These antioxidants can also help protect your body if you eat them. On top of that, the peels get their strong structures from special chemical compounds and materials known as fibers. When eaten, the chemical compounds help keep you strong, and the fibers are good for your digestive system.

Cucumbers are technically a fruit! This is because they grow from the flowers of the vine, and their seeds grow on the inside.

Create a sail made of shaved cucumber, carrot, or other veggie skins!

Create boards filled with snacks, and find out what makes a fruit different from a vegetable.

You Need

- Crackers
- Cheese
- Your favorite fruits and vegetables
- Candy eyes (optional)

pepperoni

cheese

crackers

grapes

ham

cucumbers

The Tasty Turkey

bell peppers

candy eyes

cheese beak

pear half

bananas

mini waffles

blackberries

blueberries

breakfast sausages

bacon

strawberry yogurt

The Brunch 'n' Munch

maple syrup

apples

mini muffins

strawberries

hard-boiled eggs

raspberries

mini pancakes

Fruits vs. Veggies

When people refer to fruits and vegetables, they usually separate the two by taste; they tend to call sweet-tasting foods that grow on trees and bushes fruits, and savory foods that grow on or in the ground vegetables. But to a botanist, or a scientist who studies plants, what is categorized as a fruit depends on whether or not it contains seeds. In botany, fruits are the parts of a plant that contain seeds. Any other part of a plant—from its roots to its leaves to its stem—is called a vegetable.

GLOW-IN-THE-DARK GELATIN

Shine a black light on this wiggly creation and watch it glow!

You Need

- 1 (3-oz.) box lime-flavored gelatin
- 6 tablespoons sugar
- 1 cup clear juice like apple, white grape, or white cranberry
- 1 cup tonic water
- 6- to 8-oz jars
- Whipped cream (optional)
- Sprinkles (optional)
- Icing (optional)
- Candy eyes (optional)
- Black light

1. Combine gelatin powder and sugar in a large heat-proof bowl.

2. In a separate microwave-safe bowl, microwave juice on high for 1 to 2 minutes, or until the juice is hot.

3. Pour the juice into the bowl of gelatin and sugar. Whisk until completely dissolved. Slowly pour in tonic water. The mixture will fizz and foam. Mix well.

4. When the foam has subsided, pour the mixture into small jars with a ladle. Refrigerate 90 minutes. The gelatin will have the consistency of egg whites. Refrigerate another 4 hours.

5. Bring your creation into a dark room and turn on a black light to see the glow!

When the gelatin is set, add whipped cream and sprinkles. Then add some personality by "glueing" candy eyes to the gelatin jar with icing!

How does it work?

Jiggle and Glow

You've likely had gelatin before—and it probably didn't glow! But there are two important differences here: the tonic water and black light. Tonic water contains a chemical called quinine. The black light puts out a special type of energy called ultraviolet (UV) light. UV light is not visible to humans. But when this UV light interacts with quinine, the quinine glows. Why? The quinine absorbs the UV light. Then it puts it back out as a glow! This is called fluorescence. *Ooo, ahh!*

QUICK AND EASY

Find out how popcorn pops while you create the ultimate movie snack.

You Need

▸ Popcorn
▸ Butter spray (optional)
▸ Your favorite toppings

Corny Trail Mix

pretzels

dried cranberries

chocolate candies

toasted oat cereal

cheddar crackers

peanuts

Put the ingredients into a bag with popped popcorn, then shake!

Uni-Corn

marshmallows

pudding mix

sprinkles

Use butter spray to help powdery toppings stick.

Cheesy Corn

chocolate candies

Cookie Crunch

crumbled cookies

Parmesan cheese

cheddar crackers

chopped parsley

powdered ranch mix

Chippy Corn

crushed chips

How does it work?

BEHIND THE POP

Every kernel of popcorn contains starch, a type of nutrient known as a carbohydrate. And inside that starch is a bit of moisture in the form of water. When a kernel of corn gets really hot, the water inside it turns into steam. This steam makes the starch soft and flexible. It also causes pressure to build in the kernel. And if you're cooking popcorn in a bag in the microwave, this same steam causes the bag to puff up. When just enough pressure builds up—*pop!*—the kernel bursts open, releasing both the steam and the now softened starch. The exploded starch quickly cools, forming the tasty popcorn people know and love.

STICKY TREAT SUSHI

Create "sushi" treats out of rice cereal. Then do an experiment to make leftover rice cereal dance.

You Need

RECIPE
▶ 2 tablespoons butter
▶ 2½ cups marshmallows
▶ 3 cups rice cereal
▶ Parchment paper
▶ Rolling pin
▶ Pizza cutter
▶ Fruit rolls
▶ Your favorite toppings

EXPERIMENT
▶ Rice cereal
▶ 1 balloon

1. Place butter in a large microwave-safe bowl. Heat 5 seconds in the microwave and stir. Repeat until butter is melted.

2. Add marshmallows to the bowl. Heat for 15 seconds and stir. Repeat until melted. Stir in rice cereal.

3. Scoop the sticky rice onto a sheet of parchment paper. Place another sheet over it. Flatten the sticky rice with a rolling pin until it is ¼ inch thick. Remove the paper.

4. With a pizza cutter, slice the sticky rice into 1-inch-by-4-inch rectangles. Cut fruit rolls into 5-inch-long pieces.

5. Now, create sushi by rolling or wrapping a fruit roll around sticky rice and toppings.

Wrap It

Roll It

Now, try making the leftover rice cereal jump around as if by magic!

Jumping Cereal
Experiment

1. Scatter a handful of rice cereal on a smooth, dry surface.

2. Blow up the balloon and tie it shut. Now hold the balloon over the cereal. What happens?

3. Rub the balloon on top of your head for a few seconds. Hold it over the cereal again. Now what happens?

How does it work?

Behind the Boogie-Woogie

Static electricity is the result of a buildup of an electrical charge on an object. Every object in the universe is made up of tiny units, or particles. One type of particle is called an electron. Adding or removing electrons creates an electrical charge. When you first held the balloon over the cereal, it had no charge. But rubbing the balloon over your head, moved some of the existing electrons from your head to the balloon, giving it an electrical charge! Charges can be "positive" or "negative." The balloon's negative charge attracted the positive charge on parts of the cereal, causing them to "stand up" or even "leap" toward the balloon.

Real sushi is a Japanese dish made with rice, fish, and vegetables.

Make "wasabi" with food coloring and icing.

Make "ginger" with strips of taffy.

DECORATE IT! 75

VEGGIE INSECTS

Create celery bugs and learn all about insects.

You Need

- Cucumbers
- Tomatoes
- Celery
- Olives
- Chives
- Cream cheese or hummus

1. Cut cucumbers into circles. Slice tomatoes in half. Cut celery into 2-inch logs. Chop olives into small squares. Trim chives into 1-inch stalks.

2. Spread cream cheese or hummus onto celery with a butter knife.

3. Place cucumber and tomato on celery log. Set chives behind tomato (for antennae). Add cream cheese to help steady it.

4. Dab cream cheese on the tomatoes for eyes. Then use olive squares on the cream cheese to finish the eyes.

Inspecting Insects

The world is full of insects. In fact, they make up over 75 percent of all animal species! And though there are some 900,000 different types of insects, they all share some common features. An insect is a type of animal known as an arthropod. Other arthropods include crabs,

scorpions, centipedes, and more. Arthropods don't have skeletons inside their bodies, like humans do. Instead, they have hard, outer coverings called exoskeletons. Arthropods also have a body that is segmented, or broken into parts. And they have at least three pairs of legs.

But what sets insects apart from other arthropods? An insect's body has three segments: head, thorax, and abdomen. Unlike other arthropods, insects usually have no more than three pairs of legs. And most insects have wings!

Try different ingredients, such as turkey slices or fruit.

DRINK IT!

If you're looking for something to sip on, this chapter has just the thing!

SOUR-SWEET SIPPERS 80

FRUIT CUBES 82

FIZZY DRINKS 84

COLORFUL COCOA 86

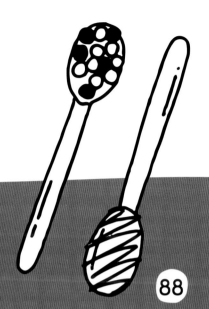

COCOA SPOONS 88

WATERMELON AGUA FRESCA 90

RAINBOW LIMEADE 92

SOUR-SWEET SIPPERS

Use sour and non–sour candies to make yummy sippers.
Then learn why sour things make your lips pucker!

You Need

▶ Ice
▶ Candies
▶ Your favorite drinks

1. Find a small, clear cup. If putting candies in the bottom of the cup, do that first.

2. Fill the cup with ice. Wedge candy pieces between the cup and the ice.

3. Mix the liquids in a separate cup, then pour the mixture over the ice.

Put the ice on top of the mini rainbow candies.

candy fish

blue sports drink

lemon–lime soda

mini rainbow candies

Fin-tastic Fishbowl

gummy dinos

watermelon sparkling water

Pucker Punch

sour gummy worms

lemon-lime soda

lemonade

Dino-mite Delight

green fruit punch

The Science of Sour

Imagine taking a big bite of a lemon—yikes! Lemons are known to be sour. So are plenty of other foods, like sour candies, cranberries, and more. Foods can taste sour when they have high amounts of a chemical substance called acid. People have strong reactions to sour foods. Why? One theory is that many acidic things in nature are harmful or poisonous to humans. What's more, human taste buds have a hard time telling which types of acid are dangerous and which aren't. Because of that, when you eat something acidic, your taste buds send a warning message to your brain. Of course, lemons are not dangerous to people—but your taste buds don't know that and send the warning anyway. As a result, your mouth might even create more saliva to help get rid of any harmful substances.

FRUIT CUBES

Add a fruity pop to ice cubes and learn how freezing works.

You Need

▸ Your favorite fruits
▸ Ice cube tray
▸ Water or seltzer

1. Wash your favorite fruits. If they're big, slice or cut them into half-inch chunks.

2. Put a few fruit pieces into each mold of an ice cube tray, then cover them with water. Freeze for at least 6 hours.

3. Add a few cubes to a glass of water or seltzer.

Chill Out!

Every item in the universe is made up of tiny units called molecules. These molecules all interact with each other to form everything you see (and even many things you don't!). Molecules also react to temperature. When a liquid is in its normal form, its molecules move at a normal pace. However, when it gets very cold, something else happens. When you get cold, you might run to grab a coat—but most liquids react in a very different way. As the molecules start to cool, they move slower and slower. Eventually, when they get cold enough, they stop moving and stay in fixed positions. This makes the liquid freeze, or form ice!

lime

raspberries

Try different fruit combos!

watermelon

lemon

grapes

cucumber

blueberries

strawberries

FIZZY DRINKS

QUICK AND EASY

Mix your own seltzer flavors. Then learn how those delightful bubbles are made.

You Need

- Seltzer (plain or flavored)
- Fruit
- Your favorite herbs

Lavender Lift

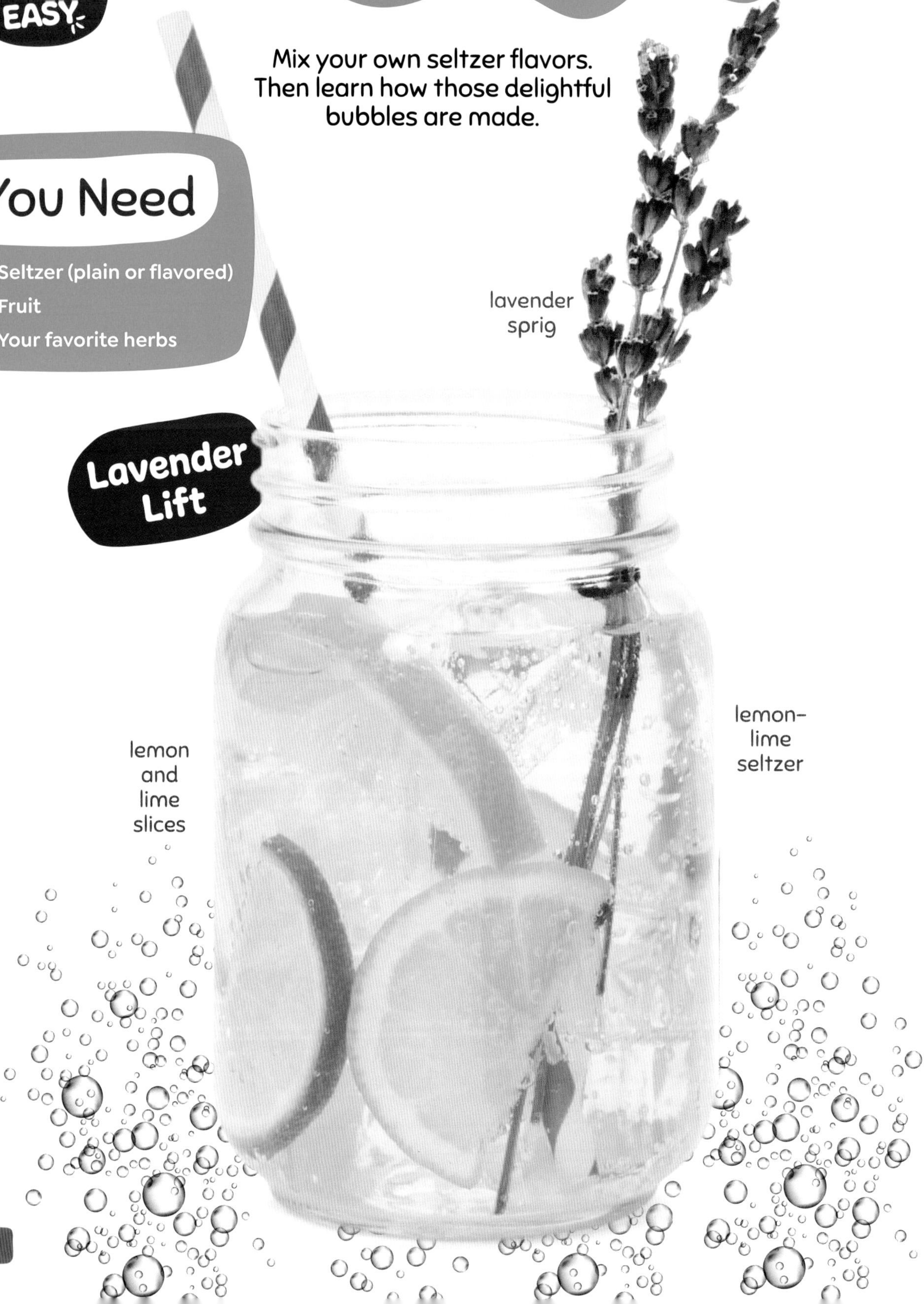

lavender sprig
lemon-lime seltzer
lemon and lime slices

Berry Blitz

mint leaves

basil leaves

Orange Spritz

berries

plain seltzer

orange slices

ginger seltzer

How Do Fizzy Drinks Get Their Bubbles?

Pop, pop, pop! Fizzy drinks are full of tiny bubbles that you can see and feel on your tongue. These bubbles are in drinks that contain dissolved carbon dioxide, which is a gas. The process of dissolving carbon dioxide into a liquid is known as carbonation.

People make fizzy drinks by pumping carbon dioxide into a container filled with the drink. They use a lot of pressure when doing this to dissolve a lot of gas in the liquid. Then they seal the container to keep in the gas. When you open a drink container—or pour a beverage from a drink dispenser—the gas escapes as fizzy bubbles to the surface. This gas is what gives these drinks their famous *pop!*

COLORFUL COCOA

Make cool cocoa drinks, then discover the science of whipped cream!

You Need

RECIPE
- Milk
- White chocolate cocoa mix
- Food coloring
- Flavored syrup (optional)
- Icing
- Whipped cream
- Your favorite toppings

EXPERIMENT
- Timer
- Heavy cream or whipping cream
- Powdered sugar

1. With an adult's help, heat milk in a microwave or in a saucepan on the stove. Stir in white chocolate cocoa mix.

2. Add 1 to 2 drops of food coloring. For extra flavor, add a few drops of your favorite flavored syrup.

3. Add icing around the rim of the mug, then add whipped cream and toppings of your choice.

whipped cream

strawberries

mini marshmallows

sprinkles

vanilla icing

red food coloring

strawberry-flavored syrup

Coat the mug's rim in frosting to make sprinkles and candies stick!

🧪 Whipped Cream Experiment

1. Grab a stopwatch or a timer. Pour heavy cream or whipping cream into a mixing bowl and add powdered sugar to taste.

2. Ask an adult to help you use an electric mixer on high to whip the cream. Start your timer. How long does it take for the cream to become stiff and fluffy?

3. Try the recipe again, but mix the cream on a lower speed setting. How much longer does it take for the whipped cream to form?

peanut butter cereal

circle candy melt with icing

caramel sauce

crushed peanut butter candies

chocolate icing

orange food coloring

Behind the Fluff

Heavy cream is a type of dairy—like milk—that contains lots of fats. In the carton or a glass, it is thick and liquid-y. But when you whip it, it becomes light, airy, and fluffy. The act of whipping, or mixing really quickly, mixes in lots of air molecules. At the same time, the beater breaks apart the fat molecules in the cream. The fat molecules re-form quickly, trapping air inside. The faster you whip, the more air you introduce, and the stiffer and fluffier the cream becomes.

COCOA SPOONS

Create hot cocoa spoons and, while stirring your drink, discover the science of how things dissolve.

You Need

- ▶ Chocolate chips
- ▶ Wooden spoons
- ▶ Parchment paper
- ▶ Your favorite toppings

1. In a microwave-safe bowl, melt chocolate chips on half power for 30 seconds.

2. Stir and repeat until fully melted.

3. Dip a wooden spoon into the melted chocolate, then set the spoon on a plate lined with parchment paper.

4. Add toppings and freeze 5 minutes or until the chocolate sets.

graham cracker crumbs + mini dehydrated marshmallows

For a flavor boost, stir these spoons into hot cocoa or another warm drink.

crushed cookies

sprinkles

butterscotch chip drizzle

candy melt drizzle

mini M&Ms

crushed caramel hard candies + sea salt

crushed cinnamon hard candies

crushed peppermints

To drizzle melted chocolate, scoop it into a sandwich bag, cut off a corner, and squeeze it out.

How Do Things Dissolve?

Some things—like the chocolate on these spoons—seem to disappear when mixed into liquid. In reality, the tiny units that make up the chocolate, called particles, have simply broken apart to mix with the water. This is called dissolving. Dissolving happens more quickly in hot water because the heat causes the chocolate and water particles to move faster and come into contact more frequently. Stirring also increases the rate at which the chocolate dissolves because it continually exposes the particles in the chocolate to the water particles that are dissolving them.

WATERMELON AGUA FRESCA

Create a refreshing drink from watermelon,
and learn to tell when the fruit is ripe.

You Need

- 6 cups seedless watermelon
- Potato masher
- Mesh strainer
- 4 cups cold water
- ¼ cup lime juice
- 1 tablespoon honey or agave

DID YOU KNOW?

Not all watermelons are red on the inside. The red or pink coloring of a watermelon comes from a special plant pigment. But watermelons can come in other colors, including yellow and even a white variety called the White Wonder!

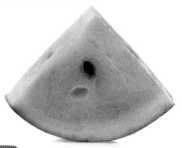

1. With an adult's help, cut a watermelon into cubes and place in a large bowl. Crush the cubes with a potato masher. Chill 30 minutes or until cool.

2. Pour the watermelon through a mesh strainer into a pitcher.

3. Mix in cold water, lime juice, and honey. Refrigerate as needed.

4. Pour the agua fresca into glasses and enjoy!

What Do a Watermelon's Markings Mean?

Outside of its juicy, red interior, a watermelon's hard shell—or rind—is famous for its striped markings. But did you know that these markings can tell you something about the watermelon? A watermelon's rind gets its coloring from a substance known as chlorophyll (see page 104). As a watermelon ripens, the chlorophyll makes the stripes a deep, dark green—and the spaces between its stripes a bright, almost yellow green. These colors let you know when a watermelon is ready to eat. Other times, the stripes can tell you what type of watermelon you are looking at. Different breeds of watermelons have different stripe patterns.

RAINBOW LIMEADE

Create a drink layered with a kaleidoscope of colors and learn about density.

You Need

- 1 cup water
- 1 cup sugar
- Lime juice
- 8 glasses
- Food coloring

DID YOU KNOW?

Rainbows can happen at night! They're called moonbows because they're made of light refracted from the moon.

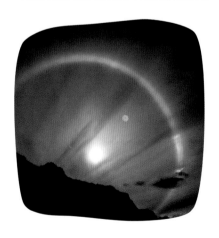

Drink Density Experiment

1. Heat water in a medium bowl in the microwave until nearly boiling (about 3 minutes). Stir in the sugar until completely dissolved and the mixture has thickened into a simple syrup.

2. Set out 6 glasses and fill each with ½ cup water. Then, mix in the following ingredients with a few drops of different colors of food coloring, as shown in the charts below.

3. To serve, fill two empty glasses each halfway with ice. In the first glass, combine the liquids from the top chart. Start by pouring in the yellow liquid. After that, pour in the green liquid. Finally, pour in the blue liquid. In the second glass, combine the liquids from the bottom chart. First pour in the purple liquid, followed by the red liquid, and finally add the blue liquid. Pour each of the liquids in slowly and carefully.

1	2 teaspoons lime juice 3 teaspoons simple syrup	Yellow food coloring
2	1 teaspoon lime juice 2 teaspoons simple syrup	Green food coloring
3	1 teaspoon lime juice 1 teaspoon simple syrup	Blue food coloring

1	2 teaspoons lime juice 3 teaspoons simple syrup	**Purple** food coloring
2	1 teaspoon lime juice 2 teaspoons simple syrup	**Red** food coloring.
3	1 teaspoon lime juice 1 teaspoon simple syrup	**Blue** food coloring

Decoding Density

How does it work?

Each layer of your drink has different amounts of simple syrup, a thick liquid made from dissolving sugar in water. The more dissolved sugar in the layer, the higher its density. The densest layer remains at bottom, while the next densest one sits above it. Finally, the least dense layer rests at the top. The differing density levels prevent layers from mixing. And because the sugar increases from top to bottom, the drink is just going to get sweeter and sweeter and sweeter as you sip!

COOK IT!

If you want a variety of recipes to help you practice your cooking skills, look no further.

BAKED EGG CUPS 96

TOP THIS 98

FANTASTIC FRIES 100

102

FLAVOR FLIPPERS

104

BROCCOLI CUPS

SILLY, STEAMY

108

OATMEAL

106

SLOPPY SLIDERS

BAKED EGG CUPS

Whip up egg cups and discover why eggs solidify when they cook.

You Need

- ▶ 4 ramekins
- ▶ 4 tablespoons heavy cream or half-and-half
- ▶ 4 large eggs
- ▶ ¼ cup shredded cheese (Gruyère or Cheddar)
- ▶ Salt and black pepper
- ▶ 2 teaspoons minced fresh chives
- ▶ ¼ cup crumbled cooked bacon or bacon bits

Different breeds of hens make different-colored eggs. Eggs can be white, brown, pink, and even blue!

1. Preheat the oven to 375°F. Place the ramekins on a baking tray and coat them with cooking spray.

2. Place 1 tablespoon heavy cream, 1 egg, and 1 teaspoon cheese into each ramekin.

3. Season with salt and pepper. Sprinkle with chives and bacon.

4. With an adult's help, bake 10 to 12 minutes for the yolk to set. Serve immediately with toast.

How Do Eggs Solidify?

When you crack open an egg, out comes a bunch of clear goop. However, when someone fries an egg, the goopy egg white turns into a solid white disk. The white part of an egg contains about 90 percent water and 10 percent protein. Uncooked, the proteins in the egg whites remain in small, compact forms. But when they come into contact with heat, the structures that keep these proteins folded up break. Now, the proteins stretch out and begin to interact with other parts of the egg white. The protein mixes with the water, forming the soft, solid whites you eat.

TOP THIS

Put your own twist on pizza and watch thermodynamics in action!

You Need

▸ Premade pizza dough or crust
▸ Your favorite pizza sauce
▸ Your favorite toppings

Margherita Pizza

mozzarella cheese

basil

tomato sauce

Behind the Melt

Mmm...how great is a pizza with ooey, gooey cheese? It's all thanks to thermodynamics, or the science of how heat moves between objects. Normally, most cheeses exist as solids due to the proteins, a type of nutrient, they contain.

But heat breaks apart these proteins. This allows the cheese molecules to move about easily, or become fluid. They aren't liquids, but they are oozy and flowing. Delicious!

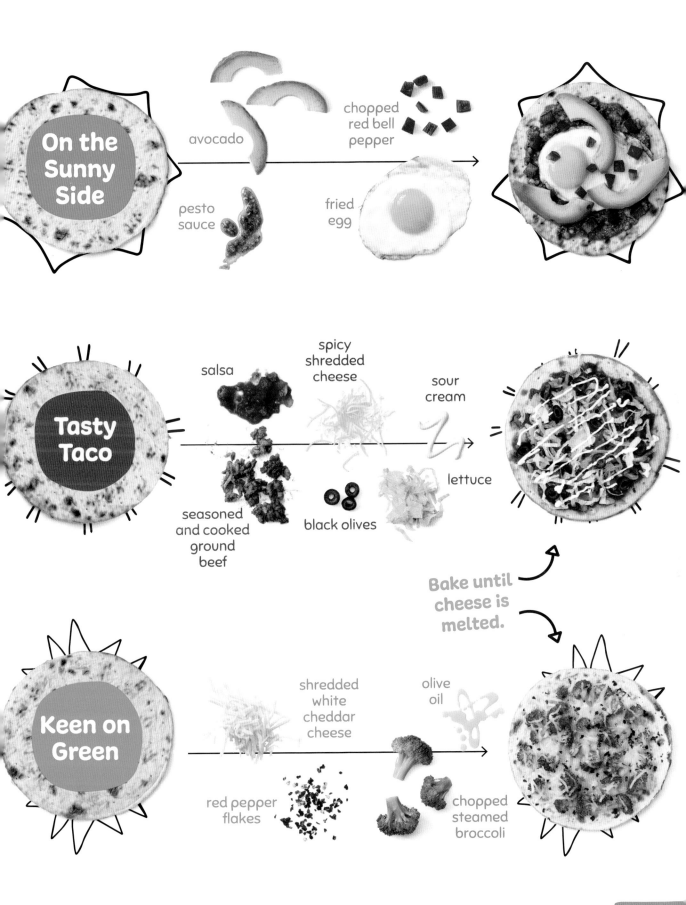

On the Sunny Side

avocado

chopped red bell pepper

pesto sauce

fried egg

Tasty Taco

salsa

spicy shredded cheese

sour cream

seasoned and cooked ground beef

black olives

lettuce

Bake until cheese is melted.

Keen on Green

shredded white cheddar cheese

olive oil

red pepper flakes

chopped steamed broccoli

FANTASTIC FRIES

Cook up some DEE-licious veggie fries. Then discover how regular potato fries are usually made.

You Need

- ½ pound vegetables of your choice, such as sweet potato, zucchini, squash, carrots, or green beans
- ¼ cup flour
- Salt and pepper
- 1 egg
- 1 tablespoon milk
- ¾ cup Panko breadcrumbs
- 3 tablespoons grated Parmesan cheese
- Parchment paper

1. Preheat the oven to 425°F. Cut the vegetables into ½-inch sticks.

2. Make 3 mixtures:
1: Flour, salt, and pepper
2: Egg and milk, beaten together
3: Breadcrumbs and Parmesan

3. Dip the veggie sticks in each bowl in order: flour mix, egg mix, breadcrumb mix.

4. Place the veggie sticks in a single layer on a baking sheet covered with parchment paper. Bake 10 to 12 minutes or until golden brown.

The Fry Factor

Your average potato fries are made in a different way from these veggie ones. They're, well, fried! Frying is a method of cooking food in a very hot pool of oil or other fats. Most frying happens in a shallow pan with a thin layer of fat. Stir-frying requires an extra-thin layer of the liquid in a superhot pan. Deep-frying, on the other hand, requires completely submerging a food in fat. In all three cases, what is happening is a transfer of heat. Fat heats up much quicker than water or air, making food cook faster. The fat also adds a rich taste to the outer surface of whatever is cooking. Yum!

FLAVOR FLIPPERS

Build tasty triangular wraps. Then discover why onions make you cry.

You Need

▸ Wraps (tortillas)
▸ Your favorite ingredients

1. Make a cut just to the center of a wrap.

2. Place a different ingredient in each of the four sections. Then fold the wrap as shown. Eat it hot or cold!

Flip it over.

Flip it up.

Flip it down.

Cluck Deluxe

tomatoes

lettuce

tomato-basil tortilla

chicken salad

bacon

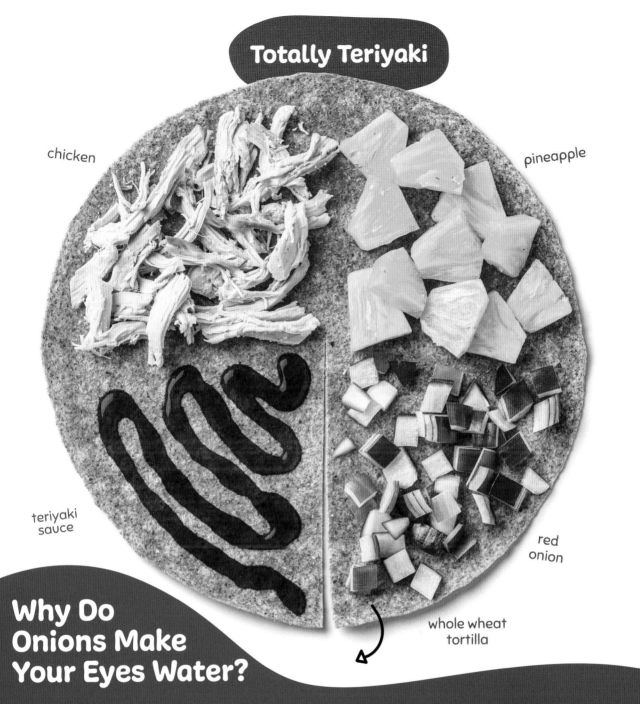

chicken

pineapple

teriyaki
sauce

red
onion

whole wheat
tortilla

Why Do Onions Make Your Eyes Water?

Cutting into a tasty onion isn't always pleasant—in fact, it can make your eyes sting and water! Inside each one of an onion's cells is a special substance known as an enzyme. An enzyme's usual purpose is to speed up chemical reactions. When someone cuts into an onion, its cells break open and the enzymes are free to do their job. Once released, they cause some of the other chemicals in the onion to form a new compound called syn-propanethial-S-oxide. This chemical is so light that it floats through the air, right into contact with the eyes of anyone near the onion being chopped. The chemical irritates the eyes, causing them to produce tears to wash away the chemical. This chemical isn't dangerous, but it can cause an unpleasant burning feeling. For many people, though, the annoyance is worth it for a yummy onion-filled dish.

BROCCOLI CUPS

Make a tasty broccoli recipe, and discover what gives broccoli its green color.

You Need

- ▶ **Muffin tin**
- ▶ **Paper muffin liners**
- ▶ **Cooking spray**
- ▶ **Round crackers**
- ▶ **2 cups broccoli, cooked**
- ▶ **2 eggs**
- ▶ **1 cup shredded cheddar cheese**
- ▶ **1 cup diced ham**

1. Preheat the oven to 350°F. Line a muffin tin with liners and spray with canola oil. Drop a cracker in the bottom of each liner.

2. Crush 20 crackers with your hands or a rolling pin.

3. With an adult's help, finely chop the cooked broccoli with a blender or food processor. Transfer to a large bowl. Mix with eggs, cheese, ham, and crushed crackers.

4. Scoop the mixture into the muffin liners and bake for 12 minutes or until the tops are golden brown.

Going Green

Broccoli almost looks like a miniature tree—and it's even green like most trees! That's thanks to a chemical called chlorophyll. Chlorophyll gives green veggies like broccoli and leafy greens their coloring. It is also one of the most important chemicals found in vegetables, trees, and other plants. Chlorophyll helps plants turn sunlight into energy in a process known as photosynthesis. During this process, chlorophyll absorbs energy from sunlight. It then uses this energy to create nutrients for the plant.

The part of the broccoli plant that we eat is actually the flower! Each individual cluster of green buds is called a floret.

What other veggies could you add or substitute in this recipe?

SLOPPY SLIDERS

Try a twist on a sloppy joe!

Buffalo Joe

You Need

▶ Slider buns
▶ Your favorite meat or veggie base
▶ Your favorite sauce
▶ Your favorite toppings

slider bun

cooked shredded chicken

wing sauce

blue cheese

celery

1. Cook chicken, veggie burger, ground pork, or another base. Shred or crumble as needed.

2. Toss it in sloppy joe sauce or a sauce of your choice.

3. Assemble on slider buns and add toppings.

Why Is Blue Cheese Blue?

When a cheesemaker creates cheese, they start by adding special bacteria and enzymes to milk (see page 152). To make blue cheese, however, the cheesemaker also adds a bacteria called *Penicillium*—a type of mold! Don't worry; this mold is completely harmless to humans. In fact, it gives blue cheese its unique smell and taste. Historians think that blue cheese first came about by accident hundreds of years ago, when mold may have grown on cheese stored in caves. Today, people add *Penicillium* on purpose by creating small holes in the cheese and popping in the mold. Yum!

Veggie Joe

DID YOU KNOW?

Some believe the name "sloppy joe" comes from a cook named Joe who added tomato sauce to his "loose meat" sandwiches.

red onion

coleslaw

whole wheat bun

sloppy joe sauce

crumbled veggie burger

Tropical Joe

slider bun

red cabbage

sloppy joe sauce

pineapple

cooked ground pork

cooked bacon

SILLY, STEAMY OATMEAL

Heat up a bowl of oatmeal and add toppings. Then find out why food steams when it's hot.

You Need

▸ **Oatmeal**
▸ **Your favorite toppings**

cheese

Buzzy Bee

hard-boiled egg

cherry tomatoes

chives

mango

Kitty Whiskerton

blueberries

strawberry

coconut chips

Hootie McBird

bananas
blueberries
clementines

dried mango

sliced almonds

Why Does Food Steam When Hot?

The steam you see rising from hot foods shows that heated water is escaping into the air.

Almost all our foods contain water. We usually think of water in its liquid form. But, like other substances, it can take the form of a solid, liquid, or gas. Water freezes to form a solid (ice) and

evaporates to form a gas (water vapor).

Water evaporates around us all the time without our noticing it, such as when spilled water dries up.

When we heat a food, we raise its temperature, along with the temperature of the water it contains. As more of

the heated water molecules change from liquid form to gas, the heated water vapor escapes from the food.

Then, as it hits cooler air, the water vapor turns back into tiny liquid water droplets in the air. We see this "condensation" as steam.

PLAY WITH IT!

If you want an an excuse to play with your food,
you're gonna love this chapter.

112 DELICIOUS DINO DIG

114 WATERMELON PIZZA

115 INSTANT ICE SLUSHIE

116 WINDOWSILL GARDEN

118 DINO SPACE NUGGETS

YUMMY GUMMY SLIME 120

BANANA POPS 122

APPLE CINNAMON

OVERNIGHT OATS 126

124 **STACK 'N' SNACK KEBABS**

128 **CRACKLING MONSTER PUPPETS**

DELICIOUS DINO DIG

Set up a yummy excavation and use kitchen tools to dig out edible treasures.

You Need

- White chocolate chips
- Mini marshmallows
- Pretzel sticks
- Dino foot-shaped cookie cutters (optional)
- Wide, chewy granola bars
- Chocolate granola
- Crispy rice cereal
- Chocolate graham crackers, crushed
- Yogurt-covered raisins
- Dinosaur gummies
- Green sprinkles
- Kitchen tools for "excavating"

1. **Make dino bones:** Melt chocolate in a medium bowl in the microwave. Press a marshmallow onto both ends of each pretzel stick. Dip pretzel sticks with marshmallows into melted chocolate until they are evenly coated and resemble dinosaur bones. Place them on a plate and refrigerate until the chocolate hardens.

2. **Make dino footprints:** Use a cookie cutter or knife to cut granola bars into the shape of dinosaur feet.

3. **Make dirt:** On a rimmed baking sheet, toss granola, cereal, and graham cracker crumbs together until combined. Nestle the pretzel dinosaur bones, yogurt-covered raisins, and dinosaur gummies into the granola mixture. Top with sprinkles to resemble grass.

4. Using a pastry brush, toothpicks, or spoons, dig and brush away "dirt" to reveal "dinosaur fossils"!

DID YOU KNOW?

Humans have been finding dinosaur fossils for thousands of years. People once thought the fossils belonged to dragons! In the 1800s, scientists began to understand that they were long-extinct reptiles.

Try making different kinds of fossils with your ingredients. You could try making "plants," "shells," and even "teeth" for your dig.

Finding Fossils

A paleontologist is a scientist who studies extinct animals like dinosaurs. Many paleontologists study fossils—the preserved remains or traces of something that was once alive. Paleontologists search for fossilized bones, tracks, plants, and more.

Many times, fossils need to be carefully removed from the earth to be studied. Paleontologists use tools like small hammers, chisels, and brushes to carefully excavate, or dig, them up. Sometimes, paleontologists work in the field, or in the area of land where the fossil was found. Other times, they dig up a large chunk of earth containing a fossil, and ship that to a research lab. There, experts use tools like a mini jackhammer, dental picks, and paintbrushes to reveal the fossil.

WATERMELON PIZZA

QUICK AND EASY

Make watermelon pizza and learn how much water is really in a watermelon.

You Need

▶ Watermelon
▶ Greek yogurt
▶ Your favorite fruits

1. Cut watermelon into triangular slices.

2. Pat dry.

3. Add yogurt and fruit on top.

Pretend you run a watermelon pizzeria and serve these yummy slices to friends and family!

peach

strawberries

pineapple

blackberries

blueberries

raspberries

kiwi

mint leaves

grapes

Sipping Slices

Why does a slice of watermelon feel so refreshing in the summer? The answer is right in the name—it contains a lot of water. In fact, a watermelon is about 92 percent water! But if you're not a fan of watermelon, don't fret. Lots of other fruits and vegetables—like cucumbers, tomatoes, cantaloupe, strawberries, celery, and more—hold high amounts of water too.

A watermelon is...

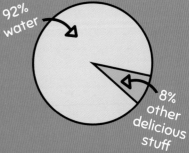

92% water

8% other delicious stuff

INSTANT ICE SLUSHIE

Try this experiment and watch a slushie form before your eyes!

 Ice Slushie Experiment

You Need

- Food coloring (optional)
- Plastic bottle of purified water
- Pan
- Ice cubes

1. If you wish, add a drop of food coloring to purified (bottled) water.

2. Place the purified water bottle on its side in a freezer for 1½ to 2 hours. When it's ready, the bottle will look a little bit hazy, but don't let the water freeze.

3. Place ice cubes in a pan. Carefully remove the water bottle from the freezer.

4. Slowly pour the water over the ice cubes. Watch as a slushie forms!

How does it work?

Ice-Cold Crystals

Two things have to happen for the water to freeze:
1. The water has to cool to below 32°F. This is called supercooling.
2. A few water molecules have to "start" an ice crystal by clinging to something solid, such as an ice cube (as shown here), dust in the water, or the rough edge of a surface. Once a few water molecules stick to an ice starter, they link together, forming crystals, or ice.

WINDOWSILL GARDEN

Instead of tossing your vegetable ends into the compost or trash, follow these easy steps to keep the food growing.

You Need

▸ Veggie scraps
▸ Jars
▸ Water
▸ Sunlight

1. Cut off the base of a vegetable. This will be your scrap. (It should be about 1 or 2 inches tall.)

2. Place the scrap in a small glass jar or shallow dish, root-side down. Add just enough water (an inch or less) to cover some of the base. Then, put the jar on a sunny windowsill and change the water every 2 to 3 days.

You won't regrow whole carrots, but you can grow the greens for salads and soups.

3. After a week or 2, you'll see growth. After a few weeks, you'll be able to clip pieces from the top and enjoy a windowsill salad!

Grow On

Gardening from scraps may seem simple, but there is a lot of science going on. Scrap gardening can involve planting or nurturing the seeds of the fruit or veggie you just ate. The seeds then use the nutrients around them to develop into brand-new plants! In other cases, a damaged plant regrows itself into a full plant. This is known as regeneration. It may seem incredible for humans, but many plants and animals have this amazing ability. For regeneration to take place, part of the plant must be missing (or eaten!), and part—including the roots—must still remain. As long as the roots are still delivering nutrients, the plant can start to regrow. To do this, the plant's tiny building blocks known as cells work to grow new cells and replace the missing parts.

DINO SPACE NUGGETS

Make an out-of-this-world scene with dinosaur-shaped nuggets, and discover the real deal behind food eaten in space.

cheese

cucumber

cheese ring

peppers

kiwi

chicken nuggets

flour tortilla

Food in Space

Dinosaurs don't really blast off into space, but humans do! And when they're visiting, they still need to eat. Food sent to space has to be able to stay fresh a long time before it is eaten. For this to happen, people often dehydrate, or take the water out of, the food. This prevents bacteria from breaking down the food or causing it to rot. Dehydrating food also makes it lighter, which is important for when it's loaded on a packed spacecraft! Later, water can be added back to the food, rehydrating it.

Food in space also needs to be safe for the astronauts. When there is very little gravity, tiny crumbs can float away and into machines, causing damage. Because of this, astronauts don't use bread on space stations—instead, they use tortillas.

Food can also taste a bit bland in space, possibly because of the effects of weightlessness on the human body. So some astronauts use lots of hot sauce!

YUMMY GUMMY SLIME

Create edible slime out of gummy candies.

You Need

- ▶ 1 teaspoon cooking oil
- ▶ ½ cup gummy candy
- ▶ 2 tablespoons powdered sugar
- ▶ 4-plus tablespoons cornstarch

1. In a microwave-safe bowl, combine the oil and the gummy candy. Heat 15 seconds or until melted.

2. Stir in the powdered sugar and 4 tablespoons cornstarch.

3. Let the mixture cool at least 10 minutes.

4. To make the slime less sticky, add more cornstarch, one tablespoon at a time.

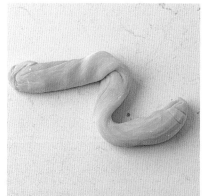

DID YOU KNOW?

Mucus is a type of slime. Animals use mucus for lots of different things, like to keep noses dirt free and to protect themselves from predators. Parrotfish are known to make mucus bubbles that they sleep inside. This helps protect the fish from parasites.

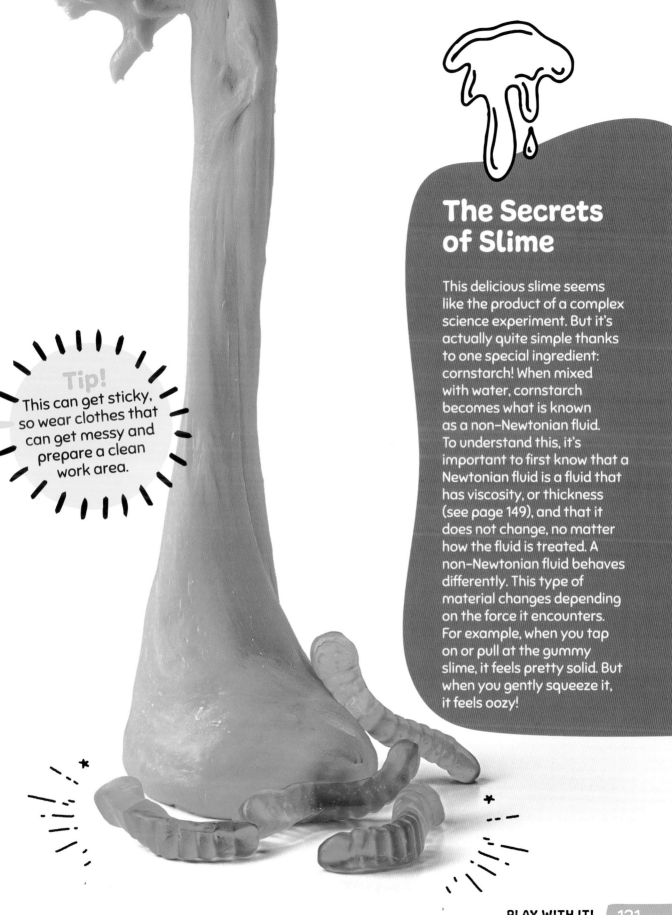

Tip!
This can get sticky, so wear clothes that can get messy and prepare a clean work area.

The Secrets of Slime

This delicious slime seems like the product of a complex science experiment. But it's actually quite simple thanks to one special ingredient: cornstarch! When mixed with water, cornstarch becomes what is known as a non–Newtonian fluid. To understand this, it's important to first know that a Newtonian fluid is a fluid that has viscosity, or thickness (see page 149), and that it does not change, no matter how the fluid is treated. A non–Newtonian fluid behaves differently. This type of material changes depending on the force it encounters. For example, when you tap on or pull at the gummy slime, it feels pretty solid. But when you gently squeeze it, it feels oozy!

BANANA POPS

Customize some delicious banana pops. Use leftover sprinkles or decorating sugar for an experiment with sound waves.

You Need

RECIPE
- ▶ Bananas
- ▶ Craft sticks
- ▶ Chocolate hummus
- ▶ Sprinkles or decorating sugar
- ▶ Your favorite toppings

EXPERIMENT
- ▶ Plastic wrap
- ▶ Cup or bowl
- ▶ Rubber band
- ▶ Plate or tray
- ▶ Sprinkles or decorating sugar (nonpareils work best)

cereal with strawberry

shredded coconut

sprinkles

1. Peel the bananas and cut each one into 3 pieces. Then stick a craft stick in one end of each banana piece.

2. Spread chocolate hummus on the bananas and roll them in your favorite toppings.

Now shake things up using your voice and extra sprinkles or decorating sugar.

 Vibrating Sprinkles & Sugar
Experiment

1. Stretch a piece of plastic wrap tight over the top of the cup or bowl. Slip the rubber band around it to keep the plastic wrap in place. Make sure it's as tight and smooth as possible.

2. Place the cup or bowl on top of your plate or tray. This will catch any sugar or sprinkles that fall off.

3. Carefully place the sugar or sprinkles on top of the plastic wrap.

4. Bring your mouth close to the edge of the cup or bowl without touching it. Hum loudly. What happens?

5. Try humming in different ways—you can hum higher or lower, and softer or louder. Do different things happen when you hum?

How does it work?

Moving and Shaking

You may have seen the sprinkles or sugar start to vibrate. What caused this? Your voice! Sounds are made up of sound waves caused by the vibrations of tiny molecules in the air. These vibrations allow humans to hear things. Deep in our ears, a thin tissue called the eardrum catches vibrations and passes sound on to the middle ear. There, tiny ear bones help magnify the sound before it travels to the inner ear. Finally, small cells called hair cells translate the sound into electrical messages, which they send to the brain. Sound vibrations can also cause other things to move. When you hummed near the plastic wrap, the sound waves from your voice caused the plastic wrap to move up and down, making the sprinkles or sugar shake and wiggle.

STACK 'N' SNACK KEBABS

QUICK AND EASY

Build yummy kebabs out of all kinds of ingredients. Before chowing down, use them in a hands-on activity about gravity.

You Need

RECIPE
- Kebab sticks
- Your favorite foods

EXPERIMENT
- Kebab sticks (with one flat end)
- Different-size food pieces

Kebab Gravity Experiment

1. Hold the kebab stick vertically on the plate, pointy end up.

2. Add the heaviest ingredients first, sliding them from the pointy top to the bottom of the stick. Keep adding ingredients, going from heaviest to lightest.

3. Try sliding the ingredients around, reordering them, adding ingredients, or taking them away.

4. When you think your kebab is ready to stand on its own, let go and see how long it can balance!

Can you make the kebab balance on its own?

Gravity Unraveled

Almost every item in the universe is made of physical material known as matter—from tiny goldfish to enormous planets like Earth. No matter the size, all objects made of matter create a force called gravity, which draws other objects to it. When it comes to small objects—like goldfish or even you!—the amount of gravity created is so small that we can't detect it. But objects with more matter create more gravity.

In this experiment, you are stacking objects affected by Earth's gravity. This gravity pulls objects toward Earth's center, keeping most things safely anchored to the planet. Gravity can also make objects fall over! But it's easier to keep things balanced and upright when you keep their center of gravity in mind. The center of gravity is where an object holds most of its weight, on average. When you create a food tower, placing the largest object on top puts the center of gravity up high, making it likely to fall over. Keeping the center of gravity low keeps the tower stable.

bread

Sandwich on a Stick

red onions

bacon

turkey

cheese

cheese

Try this gravity experiment with different kinds of kebabs. Which works best?

lettuce

roasted potatoes

sour cream

ham

Spud Skewer

cherry tomatoes

chives

APPLE CINNAMON OVERNIGHT OATS

Make overnight oats. Then do a mind-blowing "magic trick" with cinnamon, water, and soap!

You Need

RECIPE

- ½ cup old-fashioned or rolled oats
- ½ cup milk of your choice
- ½ teaspoon honey or maple syrup (optional)
- ⅛ cup yogurt (optional)
- Glass jar
- Apples
- Cinnamon

EXPERIMENT

- Shallow container
- Cinnamon
- Liquid dish soap

1. Put oats, milk, and any optional ingredients into a jar.

2. Stir, then cover with a lid and store in the fridge overnight (or at least 4 hours).

3. In the morning, add fruit and other toppings, like apples and cinnamon.

apples   cinnamon

What other fruity toppings could you add?

Now, spice up your knowledge about cinnamon with this super-cool science "trick"!

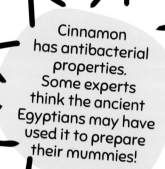

Cinnamon has antibacterial properties. Some experts think the ancient Egyptians may have used it to prepare their mummies!

 Magic Cinnamon Experiment

1. Fill the shallow container halfway with water. Sprinkle cinnamon over the water so it covers the top. What do you see?
Observe: Does the cinnamon mix with the water? Does most of it sink or float? Try mixing it with your finger–does it sink or stay floating? When you take your finger out of the water, is it covered with cinnamon?

2. Now, dip a different finger in clean water. Then slowly sink this finger into the bowl of cinnamon and water.
Observe: When you take your finger out, is it clean or covered in cinnamon?

3. Finally, rinse your hands in water. Now coat a wet finger in dish soap. Lightly touch the surface of the cinnamon in the bowl.
Observe: What happens? You should see the cinnamon moving away from your finger, as if by magic.

Cinnamon Science

During this experiment, you might have noticed that cinnamon and water don't mix. In fact, it even seems like the cinnamon touches the water as little as possible! That is because cinnamon is hydrophobic: it repels, or pushes away, water. This is why the cinnamon still seems dry even when you sprinkle it on the water! The cinnamon can peacefully rest on top of water thanks to something called surface tension, a special force that causes a layer of liquid to act almost like a solid sheet. The cinnamon floats on top of this layer and does not mix. However, when you introduce dish soap, the soap molecules lower the surface tension. But because the cinnamon is hydrophobic, it scatters away!

CRACKLING MONSTER PUPPETS

Create pretzel monsters, including one covered in Pop Rocks.
Then find out what gives Pop Rocks their crackle.

You Need

▶ **1 cup candy melts**
▶ **1 teaspoon shortening**
▶ **Pretzel rods**
▶ **Your favorite toppings**
▶ **Parchment paper**

1. In a tall, microwave-safe cup, mix candy melts with shortening.

2. Microwave on half power for 1 minute. Stir. Add more time as needed.

3. Dip pretzel rods into the mixture and lay them on parchment paper. Then have fun decorating them!

Put on a short play with your pretzel monsters before biting into them!

Behind the Bang

Pop! Pop Rocks and other popping crystal candies are famous for gently "exploding" in your mouth or in other liquids. Why does this happen? Because they're designed to! Pop Rocks are created by mixing hot sugar with a lot of a gas called carbon dioxide. When the sugar hardens, the gas is trapped inside. But when you put the candy in a liquid (including the saliva in your mouth), the hard sugar melts. Now, the gas can escape very suddenly. In fact, those fizzy feelings—and the noises you hear—are the carbon dioxide escaping!

chocolate
chips

candy
eyes

sprinkles

Pop
Rocks

129

MODEL IT!

Hands-on learners will have a blast bringing these edible science models to life!

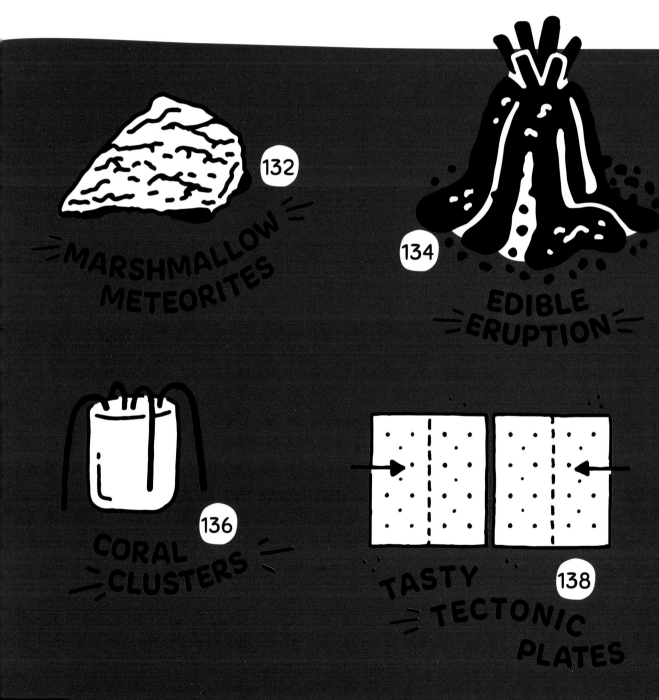

MARSHMALLOW METEORITES 132

EDIBLE ERUPTION 134

CORAL CLUSTERS 136

TASTY TECTONIC PLATES 138

**BENEATH
YOUR FEET
CUPS**

140

142

**SOLAR ECLIPSE
CRACKERS**

144

**WHIPPED CREAM
CLOUD**

145

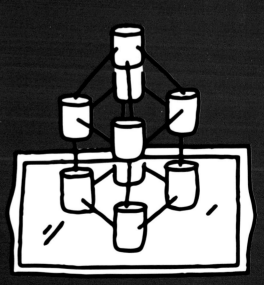

**GELATIN
EARTHQUAKE**

MARSHMALLOW METEORITES

Create a meteorite model that looks a little like the real thing—and tastes out of this world.

You Need

- ▶ Muffin tin
- ▶ Paper muffin liners (optional)
- ▶ 1 tablespoon butter
- ▶ ½ cup chocolate chips
- ▶ ¼ cup mini marshmallows
- ▶ Vanilla wafers, crushed into crumbs

1. Line a muffin tin with liners (if you are using them).

2. Melt the butter in a medium-size microwave-safe bowl. Then melt the chocolate chips in a small bowl.

3. Add a spoonful of chocolate to the butter and mix well.

4. Add the mini marshmallows and keep stirring as you sprinkle in vanilla wafer crumbs. Stop when the mixture has the consistency of cookie dough.

5. Use a spoon to scoop a lump of mixture into the muffin tin.

6. Drizzle some of the remaining chocolate on the top of your meteorites. Use the spoon to spread the chocolate to completely coat the meteorites.

7. Let the meteorite cool in the fridge.

8. When it is cool, ask an adult to help you cut it in half, and compare it to the picture of a real meteorite at the top of the next page. Try tasting the meteorite if you'd like!

CHONDRITE METEORITE

Your marshmallow meteorites are an example of a chondrite meteorite. Chondrite meteorites are little round structures made of minerals on the inside and with lumpy outsides. They're mostly made of stone.

Space Rocks

Sometimes, an asteroid or comet will smash into another object, like another space rock, a moon, or even a planet. Small pieces that break off are called meteoroids. Every so often, a meteoroid enters Earth's atmosphere. When it does, it starts to burn up, leaving a streak behind it—this is called a meteor. Most meteors completely burn away as they journey through the atmosphere. But if a meteor survives and lands on Earth, it's known as a meteorite!

DID YOU KNOW?

Earth experiences a few meteor showers every year. Two of the most famous are the Perseids, which occur in late July through the end of August, and the Leonids, which fall in November.

EDIBLE ERUPTION

With its tasty, gushing "lava," this volcanic dessert is overflowing with flavor!

You Need

- Rice cereal bars
- Red candy melts (optional)
- Milk chocolate candy melts
- Red chewing gum (optional)
- Shredded coconut (optional)
- Green food coloring (optional)
- Chocolate graham crackers (optional)
- Mentos chewy mint candy rolls
- Cola
- Red food coloring

1. Use rice cereal treats to form a small volcano, leaving plenty of empty space in the center.

2. In two separate, microwave-safe bowls, melt red candy melts (for optional lava decoration) and milk chocolate, microwaving in 30-second increments, stirring between each increment until smooth.

3. Using a spoon, spread the melted milk chocolate over the rice cereal volcano. Refrigerate 5 minutes or until the chocolate has hardened.

4. "Glue" torn pieces of gum to the volcano mouth and add a couple streams of lava with melted red candy, if you wish. Refrigerate again until candy has hardened.

5. Decorate the scene with green-dyed shredded coconut and graham cracker crumbs, if desired.

6. Place 2 to 3 Mentos inside the volcano.

7. In a cup, mix cola and a few drops of red food coloring. Pour the cola into the volcano for an eruption!

How Do Volcanoes Erupt?

Our planet is mostly made up of hot, shifting rock. The part you live on, the crust, is broken into pieces called plates that sit on the shifting rock and slowly move around. A volcano can form when these plates slide beneath one another, pull away from each other, and more.

When magma builds in volcanoes, it slowly fills the chambers deep inside. Over time, it can overflow through vents and cracks. But sometimes, the magma can get trapped or can be too thick to flow out. In these cases, gases build up inside the volcano. If the gases can't get out, pressure begins to grow. Once the pressure is too great—*boom!*—the volcano erupts, spewing lava and ash.

Try decorating your scene with dinosaur crackers or some of the "fossils" from the Delicious Dino Dig on page 112.

This eruption can get messy, so putting your volcano on a sheet tray or other pan will help contain your "lava."

CORAL CLUSTERS

Learn more about how a coral reef forms by making a bunch of individual corals, also called polyps.

You Need

- ▶ Paper plate
- ▶ White chocolate chips
- ▶ 4 large marshmallows or banana cut into 4 chunks
- ▶ Toothpick
- ▶ 24 thin pieces of red licorice (rope-style licorice works best)
- ▶ Sprinkles

1. Start building your coral reef: Set the paper plate on the table. The paper plate represents the limestone found at the base of many reefs.

2. Put the white chocolate in a bowl. Ask an adult to help you melt the white chocolate using a heat source or microwave.

3. Each marshmallow or banana chunk represents a coral polyp's body. Roll each body in the chocolate coating so the sides are covered. When the coating hardens, it's a good representation of the hard limestone skeleton that many corals have.

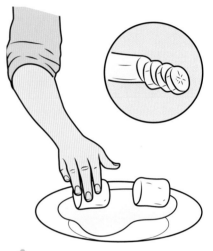

4. Place the coated marshmallows or banana chunks close to each other on the paper plate. Polyps grow very close to each other on a reef when they form colonies.

SEA FAN

Some polyps grow together to form special shapes. This is a sea fan, made of lots of polyps that spread out in a fan-like pattern. The polyps then use their tentacles to catch prey floating by.

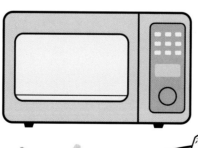

5. Use a toothpick to poke 6 evenly spaced holes in a circle around the top of each marshmallow or banana chunk.

6. Insert a thin piece of licorice in each hole. These represent a polyp's tentacles, used to pull food into the growing polyp's mouth.

7. Sprinkle a tiny bit of water on the top of the polyps, and gently add sprinkles to the top of each. These represent zooxanthellae.

8. After you're done admiring your model—eat it!

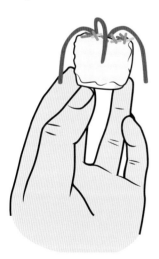

DID YOU KNOW?

Coral reefs are structures made from lots of coral polyps. These tiny marine animals grow next to one another to form reefs. The largest coral reef system on Earth, the Great Barrier Reef, can be seen from space!

What are zooxanthellae?

Zooxanthellae are tiny plantlike organisms, or algae, that live inside the coral polyp. Algae use sunlight to live and grow, like plants do. They share some of their energy with the coral. In return, the coral polyp provides a home and food for the zooxanthellae.

TASTY TECTONIC PLATES

QUICK AND EASY

Use graham crackers to re-create divergent, transform, and convergent tectonic plate boundaries.

You Need

▶ **3 paper plates**
▶ **Whipped cream, peanut butter, or frosting**
▶ **Graham crackers**

1. Using a knife, cover each paper plate with a half-inch-thick layer of whipped cream, peanut butter, or frosting. This substance represents magma (molten rock) in the mantle, the layer just beneath the crust on Earth's surface.

2. Break each graham cracker in half horizontally along the perforation in the middle. Lay the pieces of graham cracker next to each other on each plate, smooth sides touching. The graham crackers represent tectonic plates.

3. Create a divergent boundary on the first plate. Gently press down on the graham crackers as you pull them away from each other. What happens to the mantle in the middle?

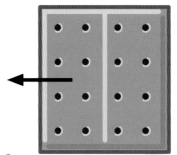

Divergent

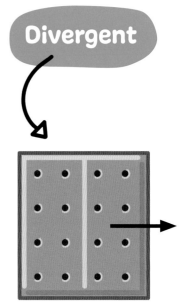

4. Create a transform boundary on the second plate. Keep the graham crackers together. With their sides touching, slowly slide one cracker up as you slide the other cracker down. How does it feel when the tectonic plates slide against each other?

Transform

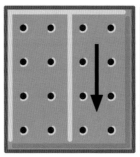

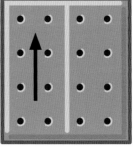

5. Create a convergent boundary on the third plate. Dip the long edge of one graham cracker in water. Put the cracker back on the plate with the soggy edge facing the other graham cracker. Gently push the two graham crackers together. Can you see the "mountains" form?

Convergent

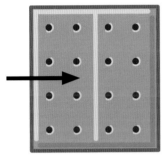 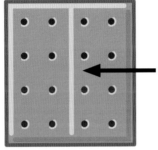

The Dirt on Tectonic Plates

Earth's crust is broken into large pieces known as tectonic plates. The plates are always in motion, but they move so slowly, it's usually unnoticeable to humans. These plates fit together like a jigsaw puzzle. An edge where two plates meet is called a plate boundary. There are three main types of plate boundaries: divergent, transform, and convergent. The plates interact with each other in different ways depending on their type of boundary. For instance, plates with convergent boundaries can collide, over time pushing up land to create mountains. Learn how plates can cause earthquakes on page 145!

DID YOU KNOW?

The Himalaya mountain range—where you can find Mount Everest, the tallest mountain on Earth—is the result of two tectonic plates crashing together. The crash first started about 55 million years ago and is still happening today!

BENEATH YOUR FEET CUPS

QUICK AND EASY

Create these dirt-free cups that explore the world right below you!

You Need

- ▶ Coconut shreds
- ▶ Food coloring

EARTH-LAYERED YOGURT CUP

- ▶ Animal crackers
- ▶ Chocolate granola
- ▶ Rainbow candies
- ▶ Vanilla yogurt

GROUNDHOG PUDDING CUP

- ▶ White chocolate chips
- ▶ Sliced almonds
- ▶ Mini chocolate chips
- ▶ Nutter Butter cookie
- ▶ Chocolate pudding
- ▶ Crumbled Oreos

animal crackers

Chocolate granola and rainbow candies (crust)

coconut shreds

Orange-dyed yogurt (outer core)

Red-dyed yogurt (mantle)

Yellow-dyed yogurt (inner core)

crust · mantle · outer core · inner core

DID YOU KNOW?

Groundhogs dig complex burrows with tunnels and rooms—they even have bathrooms!

Add a drop or two of food coloring to create colorful yogurt and coconut shreds.

sliced almonds

mini chocolate chips

Nutter Butter cookie

white chocolate chips

coconut shreds

chocolate pudding

crumbled Oreos

Inside Earth

Earth is made up of three major layers: the crust, mantle, and core. The crust is where you live—it is the outer, rocky part. It is also the thinnest layer. Below the crust is the mantle. Scientists divide the mantle into two parts: upper mantle and lower mantle. The upper mantle is made of semiliquid, molten rock. Below it, the lower mantle is made of solid superheated rock. Finally, the center of Earth contains the core. Scientists also break the core into two parts, called the outer core and inner core. The outer core is a liquid layer of floating, superheated metals. The inner core is even hotter, but is a solid metal ball because of the pressure pushing down on it.

SOLAR ECLIPSE CRACKERS

QUICK AND EASY

Create a "solar eclipse" right in your home with this snack.

You Need

- ▶ **Cut cucumber**
- ▶ **Round crackers**
- ▶ **Cream cheese**

1. Cut a cucumber into slices. Place these on a plate.

2. Lay out a row of 6 round crackers. Place a cucumber slice on top of each cracker.

3. Open the cream cheese. Leave the first cucumber slice with nothing on it. This represents the sun before a solar eclipse. Use a table knife to cover the last cucumber slice with cream cheese. This represents the sun when it's totally eclipsed.

4. Using the picture below to help, spread cream cheese on the middle four slices to represent how the shape of the sun appears to change during a solar eclipse.

5. Make sure the crackers are arranged correctly, and then eat your way through a solar eclipse!

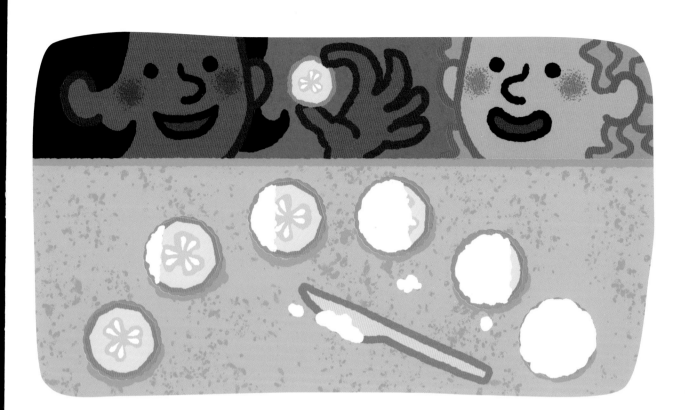

WHAT IS A SOLAR ECIPSE?

When the moon orbits Earth, sometimes it passes directly between Earth and the sun. When this happens, the moon blocks the sun's light from getting to Earth, making it look like the sun has gone dark. This is a solar eclipse. During a solar eclipse, the moon can look like it is either blocking all of the sun or only a portion. Whether you see a total eclipse or a partial one depends on where you are located on Earth in relation to the sun at the time of the event.

WHIPPED CREAM CLOUD

Make a whipped cream "cloud" that "rains down" food coloring!

You Need

- **Lemonade**
- **2 glasses**
- **Food coloring**
- **Whipped cream (from a can)**
- **Eyedropper, straw, or plastic pipette**

1. Pour half a cup of lemonade into a glass.

2. Mix a few drops of food coloring into the lemonade. This is your "rain."

3. Fill another glass or jar three-fourths full with lemonade.

4. Squirt the whipped cream into the glass or jar with the plain lemonade until it is a little higher than the top. This is your "cloud."

5. Use the eyedropper, straw, or pipette to draw up some of the rain.

6. Gently drizzle the rain on the whipped cream cloud. Wait a minute, and watch.

7. Add more rain to the cloud until you see color in the jar. You've made drinkable rain!

DID YOU KNOW?

Raindrops aren't tear-shaped: they start out like round balls, and then become the shape of a jelly bean or kidney bean as they fall and collide with other drops.

How Does Rain Fall from Clouds?

The whipped cream can hold on to, or absorb, some of the colored water. After a while, though, it can't hold anymore. When this happens, the water trickles through the cloud and falls into the water below.

Clouds form when the air is saturated with water vapor. The tiny drops that make up a cloud sometimes stick together. Gravity pulls on bigger drops more than on smaller drops. Eventually, enough drops stick together to form drops big enough that gravity makes them fall to the ground.

GELATIN EARTHQUAKE

Build an earthquake-proof building out of marshmallows and toothpicks.

You Need

▸ **Packet of gelatin**
▸ **Toothpicks**
▸ **Mini marshmallows**

Tip!
Shorter buildings are more stable than taller ones. Triangles add strength to the base.

Quake-Proof Building Experiment

1. With an adult's help, prepare the gelatin by following the instructions on the package. Pour the gelatin onto the cookie sheet. Refrigerate until the gelatin is firm.

2. Use the toothpicks and mini marshmallows to build 5 structures of different shapes and sizes. You can cut the toothpicks with scissors if you'd like to use smaller pieces. But you must use the same number of toothpicks and marshmallows in each of the structures.

3. Examine your finished structures. Predict which structures will stand the longest during an earthquake.

4. Put your predictions to the test. Place the first structure on the sheet of gelatin. Shake the cookie sheet back and forth. Keep time to see how long it takes for the structure to fall.

5. Repeat with the other structures. Be sure to shake equally hard on each try.

How Do Earthquakes Happen?

As tectonic plates (see page 139) move, they crash together, slip over each other, pull apart, and slide alongside one another. Most of the time, you can't feel the plates moving. However, the plates sometimes get stuck when they come into contact. These places are called plate boundaries. When the plates grind against each other, it causes resistance—or friction. When the plates get stuck due to friction, pressure starts to build enough force for the plates to come unstuck and keep moving. This force causes a ripple of energy that makes the ground shake—an earthquake.

RE-CREATE IT!

If you'd rather whip up your favorite foods than buy them from the store, you'll enjoy making these recipes from scratch.

CREATE YOUR OWN BUTTER 148

HOMEMADE KETCHUP 149

DIY ICE CREAM 150

COTTAGE CHEESE & CHEESY NOODLES 152

CHOCOLATE CHIP COOKIES 155

SALAD DRESSING 154

CREATE-YOUR-OWN BUTTER

Whip up some butter from scratch, then discover the science behind your creamy creation!

You Need

- 1 cup heavy whipping cream
- 1 plastic container with a screw-on lid

Behind the Butter

Humans have been making and enjoying butter for some 10,000 years. And why not? It's pretty easy! One of the simplest ways to make butter starts with cream, which is a layer of milk with a high fat content. First, a person begins to churn the cream. This means that they agitate (mix forcefully) the cream for a long while. Normally, the fat in the cream is separated by thin barriers called membranes. However, as the cream mixes, these membranes break open. Now, the sticky fat begins to clump together. The butter maker then removes these clumps and rinses them before blending them together to be smooth and creamy. *Voilà*, butter!

1. Pour the whipping cream into the plastic container. Screw on the lid tightly.

2. Toss, shake, and roll the container for 30 minutes until the cream separates into a liquid (buttermilk) and a solid (butter).

3. Pour out the buttermilk.

4. To rinse the butter, add 1 cup cold water, swirl it around, and pour the water out.

Tip! For step 2, play hot potato or another fun tossing game with a friend while shaking the container.

HOMEMADE KETCHUP

Create your own ketchup and learn about viscosity in food.

You Need

- ½ cup tomato paste
- 3 tablespoons white vinegar
- 2 tablespoons maple syrup
- ¼ teaspoon salt
- ¼ teaspoon allspice

1. Whisk together tomato paste, vinegar, and syrup.

2. Add salt and allspice. Stir.

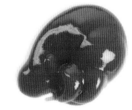

Catch Up with Ketchup

Have you ever turned a glass ketchup bottle upside down and had nothing come out? Or, have you ever squeezed a plastic ketchup bottle and had the ketchup shoot out everywhere? Both of these events are caused by ketchup's viscosity, or thickness. The viscosity of ketchup does not always stay the same. Instead, it changes depending on how much force, or pressure, acts on it (see page 15). When ketchup is in a glass bottle, there is no way to apply pressure, so the ketchup stays thick—and trapped in the bottle! But in a plastic bottle, you can gently squeeze the ketchup. This makes it act more like a liquid and come out right away.

DIY ICE CREAM

Try this hands-on recipe to learn how ice cream forms.

You Need

- ▶ **1 cup whole milk**
- ▶ **¼ cup sugar**
- ▶ **½ teaspoon vanilla**
- ▶ **1 quart-size zipper freezer bag**
- ▶ **1 gallon-size zipper freezer bag**
- ▶ **20 cups ice**
- ▶ **1½ cups rock salt (available in some supermarkets)**
- ▶ **Winter gloves (optional)**

1. Put milk, sugar, and vanilla in the quart-size freezer bag. Squeeze out the air, then zip the bag completely closed. (If it is not sealed tightly, you will end up with salty milk.)

2. Place the small bag in the large bag.

3. Pack ice almost to the top of the large bag.

4. Ask an adult to pour 1 cup of the rock salt on top of the ice. Zip the large bag completely closed.

5. Toss the heavy bag back and forth for 5 minutes. It's best to do this outside in case anything drops or opens. You may also want to wear gloves because your hands will get cold.

How Do Ice Cream Headaches Happen?

Scientists aren't totally sure why ice cream headaches, also known as "brain freezes," happen. However, they think it might have to do with the blood vessels near the back of your mouth. When you slurp up a chilly food or drink, it passes across the roof of your mouth and back of your throat. In these areas, you have lots of small blood vessels, which are the veins, arteries, and capillaries that carry blood around your body. When something very chilly touches these blood vessels, the cold causes them

6. Inside, open the large bag and drain out any excess water. Don't pour it on grass or other plants—salt water will kill them.

7. Have an adult add the rest of the rock salt and as much ice as will fit. Seal the bag again, then toss it back and forth for 5 more minutes outside.

8. Scoop your ice cream into a bowl and add your favorite toppings like cherries, sprinkles, whipped cream, and more!

If your ice cream is still looking a little runny, seal everything back up and toss it around for a few more minutes.

to squeeze suddenly. Then, once the cold item slides down your throat, the vessels warm up and quickly relax. Some scientists think that this can cause discomfort because the process sends a lot of blood to your brain at once. Others think that the unpleasant feeling might also come from the vessels squeezing and relaxing so quickly, which your brain interprets as pain.

The good news is that ice cream headaches are not dangerous, and they go away very quickly. You can try speeding them along by pressing your tongue or thumb against the roof of your mouth or drinking warm water.

RE-CREATE IT!

COTTAGE CHEESE & CHEESY NOODLES

Create cottage cheese from scratch. Then use your creation to make a delicious noodly dish.

You Need

- ▶ **4 cups milk**
- ▶ **Instant-read thermometer**
- ▶ **2 tablespoons vinegar or lemon juice**
- ▶ **Cheesecloth or non-terry tea towel**
- ▶ **Pinch of fine sea salt, or to taste**

1. Ask an adult to boil the milk in a medium saucepan until the temperature reaches 190°F. Remove from the heat.

2. Add vinegar or lemon juice and stir gently until curds start to form. Cover it and set it aside until cool enough to handle, about 30 minutes.

3. Line a fine-mesh strainer with cheesecloth. Place over a large mixing bowl to catch the liquid, which is called whey.

4. Scoop the curds into a lined strainer with a slotted spoon. Drain for 30 minutes, or until the dripping stops.

5. Rinse the cheese curds with cold running water. Twist the cheesecloth into a ball and squeeze out any excess liquid. Unwrap curds into a bowl. Stir in salt to taste.

Creating Curdle

What exactly is cottage cheese? It's curdled milk! That might not sound super appealing at first, but there's actually some very cool science at work. To make cheese, cheesemakers add special types of healthy bacteria to milk. They also add enzymes, which are substances that cause chemical reactions. Together, the enzymes and bacteria begin to break down the milk (see page 41), a process called curdling. It causes parts of the liquid milk to turn into soft, solid lumps called curds. Cheesemakers can control this process to make different types of cheeses and dairy products—including cottage cheese.

Now use your cottage cheese to make gourmet pasta right in your kitchen!

You Need

- **8 ounces corkscrew pasta**
- **1 cup cottage cheese**
- **¼ cup grated Parmesan cheese, plus more for sprinkling**
- **½ cup green peas, cooked**
- **¼ cup basil leaves**
- **¼ teaspoon garlic powder**
- **¼ teaspoon salt**
- **⅛ teaspoon ground black pepper**

1. Boil pasta and reserve ½ cup pasta water, then set it aside. In a large bowl, combine cottage cheese, Parmesan, peas, basil, garlic, salt, pepper, and 2 tablespoons pasta water.

2. With an adult's help, pour the ingredients from the bowl into a blender or food processor. Blend until smooth.

3. Pour the mixture over the pasta. Stir. Add pasta water to thin the mixture if desired.

4. Spoon the pasta into bowls. Sprinkle Parmesan cheese or basil leaves on top, if desired.

SALAD DRESSING

Stir up your own salad dressing, then discover the science behind mixing oil and water.

You Need

THOUSAND ISLAND:

- ½ cup mayonnaise
- ½ cup ketchup
- 2 teaspoons relish
- Pinch cayenne pepper
- 1 tablespoon lemon juice

RANCH:

- ½ cup buttermilk
- 2 tablespoons mayonnaise
- 2 tablespoons sour cream
- 1 teaspoon garlic powder
- 1 tablespoon white vinegar (optional for a thinner, tarter dressing)

Best Dressed

If you've ever tried to combine oil and water, you know that the two liquids do not mix. This is because oil molecules like to stick together, and water molecules like to stick together, but oil and water molecules do not like to break up and mix together.

The same goes for oil and vinegar! So how can oil and vinegar come together to form a creamy, smooth salad dressing? The answer is emulsification. This is the act of vigorously shaking, whisking, or stirring together two materials that do not

mix—also known as immiscible materials. Emulsification causes the molecules of both the oil and vinegar to break down so that tiny droplets of both liquids mix into one substance.

CHOCOLATE CHIP COOKIES

Make your own chocolate chip cookies,
then check out the buttery science behind them.

You Need

- 1 stick (½ cup) of butter or margarine, softened
- ½ cup brown sugar, firmly packed
- ¼ cup white sugar
- 1 egg
- 1 teaspoon vanilla
- 1½ cups all-purpose flour
- ½ teaspoon baking soda
- ¼ teaspoon salt
- 1 (6-oz.) package semisweet chocolate chips

1. Preheat the oven to 350°F.

2. Put the butter into a big bowl. Pour in brown sugar and white sugar. Stir this mixture until smooth and creamy. Add egg and vanilla and stir well.

3. Put the flour into a medium-size bowl. Stir in baking soda and salt.

4. Pour the flour mixture into the butter/sugar mixture. Stir well with a spoon. Then add chocolate chips to the dough.

5. Drop tablespoonfuls of dough onto a cookie sheet. Leave about two inches between each cookie. Then bake 12 to 15 minutes.

6. Using oven mitts, take the cookie sheet out of the oven. Let the cookies cool for five minutes, then remove them and place them on a wire rack or paper towels to finish cooling.

Cookie Chemistry

Your cookie goes in the oven as a gooey ball of sticky ingredients. But when it comes out, it's a semi–flat, firm, round disc. This happens in four main steps: the spread, the rise, the set, and caramelization. Heat from the oven melts the butter in the cookie, so the dough spreads out into a gooey puddle! Next, the cookie starts to puff up. Moisture in the cookie starts to evaporate in the oven's heat, pushing the dough up into a fluffy disc. Baking soda in the dough breaks down into gases, which puff up the dough even more and leave behind air pockets, making the treat flaky. Next, the cookie sets. Egg proteins firm up in the heat, solidifying the cookie. Finally, caramelization: This is when the sugars in the cookie break down, fusing together and giving the cookie its golden–brown color.

Index

Credits

Copyright © 2025 by Highlights for Children
All rights reserved.

Copying or digitizing this book for storage, display, or
distribution in any other medium is strictly prohibited.

For information about permission to reproduce selections
from this book, please contact permissions@highlights.com.

Highlights Press
815 Church Street
Honesdale, Pennsylvania 18431

ISBN: 978-1-63962-318-1
Library of Congress Control Number: 2024947670

Produced by WonderLab Group LLC: Paige Towler, science
writer; John Clifford and Tim Littleton, art direction and design;
Hillary Leo, photo editor; Katie Cederborg, fact-checker; Emily
Owens, experiment tester; Heather McElwain, copyeditor;
Susan K. Hom, proofreader; Connie Binder, indexer.

Recipe Writers: Bridget Anderson (16, 41); Bonnie Baker (40, 66,
76); Taylor Clifton (98); Dish Works Studio (12, 14, 48, 92, 112, 134);
Yesica Herd (90); Sophie Jones (24); Patricia Tanumihardja (46,
50, 64, 70, 96, 100, 108, 152); Lana R. Wieder (42).

Manufactured in Dongguan, Guangdong, China
Manufacturing date: 11/2024

Ages 7 and up

2318-01

First edition

Visit our website at Highlights.com.

10 9 8 7 6 5 4 3 2 1

Highlights.com/ShareCookingPics
SCAN ME

Photo and Illustration Credits

All Illustrations by Sebastian Abboud unless otherwise noted.
Key: GI=Getty Images, SS=Shutterstock, GCAI=Guy Cali
Associates, Inc, DWS=Dish Works Studio, RBS=Rich Brainerd
Studios

1-3: Designed by Freepik (blue background), Savany/GI (orange),
annoying.orange/GI (banana), Padgett Mozingo (kid tester);
6: atoss/GI (pepper), DWS (pyramid and limeade); 10-11: RBS
(speedy snacks), alle12/GI (tire); 12: Nick Brundle Photography/
GI (pyramids); 13: DWS (cheese and grape pyramid); 14-15: DWS
(pretzel bridge and steps), Nirian/GI (Golden Gate Bridge); 17:
Nenov/GI (strawberries); 18-19: Dan Sipple (dino marshmallow
art), Leonello Calvetti/Science Photo Library/GI (T. rex); 22:
Liudmyla Klymenko/GI (digestive system); 24-25: RBS (bagel
sandwiches and everything bagel); 26: LeventKonuk/GI
(eggs and glass); 28-29: bpablo/GI (green apple), GCAI (all
apple dippers), cako74/GI (honey); 30: cnythzl/GI (mouth);

32: bluestocking/GI (pan); 35: atoss/GI (chili pepper); 36-37:
baibaz/GI (green avocado), YuanruLi/GI (brown avocado), RBS
(avocado toast); 38-39: ttsz/GI (chemical structure), arcimages/
GI (rock candy), Vicky Lommmatzsch (rock candy steps); 40:
GCAI (banana bites and whole banana); 41: GCAI (cheesy
nibblers), Jesper Mattias/GI (cheese and machine); 47: GCAI
(grilled cheese); 49: bhofack2/GI (baked Alaska); 50: RBS (cookie
steps), Peter Carruthers/GI (cookies); 51: Squiddly/GI (maple
candy), Alain Intraina/GI (maple syrup); 52: Erik Isakson/GI
(wheat); 55: didecs/GI (mint); 56-57: MirageC/GI (marshmallows),
Robert Kirk/GI (graham crackers), IndiaPix/IndiaPicture/GI
(apple), Westend61/GI (chocolate), Dish Works Studio (s'more),
Manuel Breva Colmeiro/GI (sunshine); 61: subjug/GI (banana),
jskiba/GI (paper bag), LarryHerfindal/GI (green bananas); 64:
colematt/GI (celery and cups); 65: RBS (celery snacks); 66-67:
Jasmina007/GI (vegetables), GCAI (steps and cucumber boat);
68-69: RBS (sharing boards); 70: Cathy Scola/GI (glowing liquid);
73: threeseven/GI (kernels); 74-75: GCAI (sticky treat sushi),
claylib/GI (balloon); 76-77: GCAI (veggie insects and steps),
Antrey/GI (ant); 81: SENEZ/GI (lemon slices); 82-83: Bill Oxford/
GI (icicles), GEOFF KIDD/GI (raspberries), Adam Smigielski/GI
(blueberries), dimitris66/GI (cucumbers), SENEZ/GI (lemons),
Nenov/GI (strawberries); 84-85: alenaohneva/GI (bubbles);
87: Cathy Scola/GI (whipped cream); 88-89: RBS (cocoa
spoons and mug); 90-91: Dragos Negoita/500px/GI (yellow
watermelon), DWS (watermelon agua fresca and steps); 92:
Wirestock/GI (moonbow); 93: DWS (limeade); 96-97: GCAI
(egg cups and steps); 98-99: Brickclay/GI (thermometers),
GCAI (pizzas and ingredients); 100-101: Tashi-Delek/GI (cooking
vegetables), DWS (fries and steps); 102-103: RBS (flavor flippers);
104-105: RBS (broccoli cups and steps); 106-107: GCAI (sloppy
sliders), Science Photo Library/GI (blue cheese); 108-109:
Zakharova_Natalia/GI (oats), RBS (oatmeal bowls), posteriori/
GI (red mug); 112: benedek/GI (paleontologist); 113: DWS
(dino dig); 114: GCAI (watermelon pizza); 115: TK (slushie); 116:
Rosemary Calvert/GI (carrots); 118-119: DWS (dino nuggets),
NASA (astronauts); 120: Humberto Ramirez/GI (parrotfish); 121:
FrankRamspott/GI (slime illustration); 123: David Izquierdo
/500px/GI (colored sugar), Sudowoodo/GI (headphones);
124: Sabelskaya/GI (planet); 125: GCAI (kebabs); 127: Muluken
Mengistu /500px/GI (cinnamon); 128: GCAI (pop rocks); 129:
Mike Lowery (monsters); 132: Dan Sipple (recipe steps); 133:
Claudio Caridi/GI (meteorite), ratpack223/GI (meteorites
and Earth), Trifonov_Evgeniy/GI (night sky); 134: Beboy_ltd/
GI (volcano); 135: DWS (edible volcano); 136-137: Hal Beral/
GI (sea fan), T.M. Detwiler (coral polyp illustrations), Georgette
Douwma/GI (sea turtle), subjug/GI (sprinkles); Oxford Scientific/
GI (zooxanthellae); 138-139: Dan Sipple (graham crackers),
hadynyah/GI (mountain range), FrankRamspott/GI (plate
tectonics); 140: Kateryna Kon/Science Photo Library/GI (Earth
layers), DWS (yogurt cup); 141: Troy Harrison/GI (groundhog),
DWS (pudding cup); 142-143: Magone/GI (cream cheese),
chorboon_photo/GI (crackers), photomaru/GI (cucumbers),
Hayelin Choi (solar eclipse crackers), suman bhaumik/GI (solar
eclipse); 144: Gabriel Mello/GI (water drops), Hayelin Choi (kid);
145: Dan Sipple (gelatin structure); 148: bigacis/GI (butter),
JohnGollop/GI (buttered bread); 149: Akaradech Pramoonsin/
GI (ketchup bottle, MediaProduction/GI (ketchup splatter),
Jaromila/GI (fries); 150: subjug/GI (sundae); 151: jenifoto/GI (ice
cream cone); 152: Lena_Zajchikova/GI (cottage cheese); 153:
RBS (cheesy noodles); 154: robertsre/GI (white dipping sauce),
AtlasStudio/GI (yellow dipping sauce), Creative Crop/GI (salad);
155: EasyBuy4u/GI (cookies).